"What else would you like in a wife?"

"Let's see." Byrne stood looking down at her. "A woman who could run on her own efficiency. A woman I could absolutely trust. A woman I'd be lost without. A woman with the sweetest smile. The softest mouth. Tender, loving, concerned. A woman who wants children. Our children."

"You want a lot." There was the faintest tremble in her voice.

He shrugged his wide shoulders. "Marriage has to be the biggest decision in life."

"Oh, Byrne, look. A falling star!" Toni put out her hand, caught his sleeve, heart leaping.

"All the brighter in the falling. You'd better make a wish."

Let him love me. The thought came spontaneously from deep within her.

Dear Reader,

Welcome to

Everyone has special occasions in their life—times of celebration and excitement. Maybe it's a romantic event, an engagement or a wedding—or perhaps a wonderful family occasion, such as the birth of a baby. Or even a personal milestone—a thirtieth or fortieth birthday!

These are all important times in our lives and in **The Big Event!** you can see how different couples react to these events. Whatever the occasion, romance and drama are guaranteed!

We'll be featuring one book each month from May to August 1998, bringing you terrific stories from some of your favorite authors. And, to make this miniseries extraspecial, **The Big Event!** will also appear in the Harlequin Presents® series.

This month celebrate not one, but two weddings in Margaret Way's *Beresford's Bride*, and look out next month for Jessica Hart's *Birthday Bride*.

Happy Reading!

The Editors

P.S. Follow the series into our Presents line in September with Kathryn Ross's *Bride for a Year*.

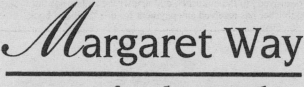

Margaret Way

Beresford's Bride

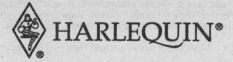

TORONTO • NEW YORK • LONDON
AMSTERDAM • PARIS • SYDNEY • HAMBURG
STOCKHOLM • ATHENS • TOKYO • MILAN • MADRID
PRAGUE • WARSAW • BUDAPEST • AUCKLAND

ISBN 0-373-03507-1

BERESFORD'S BRIDE

First North American Publication 1998.

CHAPTER ONE

AT SEVENTEEN she was as pretty as a Persian kitten. At twenty-two she was dazzling, the sort of shining ash-blonde men couldn't take their eyes off.

Zoe all over again.

Then again, she wasn't, he mused, as the image of the mother was superimposed on his mind. She was several inches taller, her body very willowy and slender where Zoe's petite frame was almost lush. But the same familiar sex appeal was there. The same chemistry that left men dazzled. She was walking away from the elevator with two good-looking guys about his own age flanking her, obviously paying court. They were doing the talking, she was doing the laughing, one arm raised to fan her long waterfall of hair.

He lost seconds.

The one thing he hadn't counted on was his own re-action. It shocked him as much as some blinding en-counter. His stomach muscles clenched and the blood in his veins began a slow burn. How too damned extraor-dinary! He gave himself a moment to regain his ha-bitual detachment. This was young Toni, remember? Antoinette Streeton. He had known her all her life even if she had been too young to catch his attention.

Toni was the only daughter of the late Eric Streeton and the notorious Zoe Streeton Von Dantzig LeClair. The Streetons had owned and worked Nowra Station since the turn of the century. Nowra was their nearest neighbour some hundred miles to the northeast, and Eric

Streeton had been a lifelong friend of his father and un-
cles. In fact, Eric Streeton had been best man at his
parents' wedding. The entire family had taken it very
hard when Eric Streeton had lost the battle with septicemia a few years before. A deep gash ignored until it
was too late. That was Eric. At that time he and his son,
Kerry, had been on their own. Zoe had walked out on
him when the children were adolescents, returning to
sweep Antoinette off to Paris after her final year at
boarding school. It was supposed to have been a treat,
six months at most. Antoinette stayed with her mother
for the best part of five years. Neither had come home
for Eric Streeton's funeral. They'd been too busy cruis-
ing the Greek islands with one of Zoe's admirers, later
to become her second husband, Von Dantzig. These days
Zoe was on to *numero tre*. That was the Frenchman. He
really didn't want to think about it, feeling the same
quiet rage now as he had then, the same *sadness* at the
way Eric had been treated. The vast Outback, sparsely
populated but closely linked, had felt the same way.
Now Zoe's daughter was walking toward him, the light
catching some sparkling thread in her short evening
dress. It was a very simple garment, figure-skimming,
but a showcase for her lovely body and limbs. Her years
in Paris showed. She looked enormously chic, finished
in a way other beautiful young women of his acquaintance were not. The two guys were waving goodbye like
old friends, one whipping out a small black notebook
and scribbling something on a page. A telephone number, address? God, shades of Zoe! It touched a raw
nerve.

She was moving into the main foyer, drawing all eyes.
She must have felt his observation because her head
turned quickly as though she was following a beam. He

stood up, abandoning the evening paper, trying to dispel the odd mood that had settled over him.

He was even more formidable than she remembered, tall, lean, darkly, aggressively handsome. A man's man but with a powerful sexuality that made him dangerous to women, like the ironic sparkle in his beautiful rain-coloured eyes. She'd have known him anywhere. Anywhere in the world. For a moment on seeing him she felt a heart-stopping sensation akin to narrowly missing being run over. She found it hard to breathe. It was so strange to face Byrne Beresford again, with his bright aura of excitement, glamour, power. This was the man who ruled a cattle empire with an iron hand. The man she had fantasised about as a profoundly impressionable and romantic teenager. Not that he had ever looked at her except as Kerry's kid sister. Not solid and focused like Kerry. Potentially another Zoe, a woman as insubstantial as she was lovely, a woman with a habit of wrecking lives. This was Byrne Beresford, the man she had known all her life and would *never* know.

He was moving purposefully towards her with all the natural grace of some powerful big cat. Six foot three of taut energy that crackled loose like electricity, elegant in the city clothes he wore like a patrician, but something about him, the vigour, the vitality, the deep tan and the far-seeing eyes proclaimed four walls couldn't contain him. He was what he was, a member of the landed establishment, a cattle baron of influence and power. A man impossible for anyone to ignore, much less a member of the opposite sex.

"Byrne!" She took a deep breath and put out her hand. He not only took it but bent his dark head to brush his mouth against her cheek. A smooth slide that had a

profound effect on her. She not only felt it on her face
but right through her body.

"Antoinette, welcome home. How are you? You
haven't changed at all." Which was absurd. She had
blossomed like some wondrous rose. She had a perfect
creamy skin with a light fragrance that seemed to engulf
him. Damn. It rattled him, being so effortlessly charmed.

"How wonderful to see you! It's been years!"

"Five next March," he responded, regarding her.
"You're all grown up." But definitely off-limits, even
if she was far more than he was prepared for.

"Paris has been good to me. How is everyone? You
must tell me."

"Everyone's fine," he told her. "Why don't we go
in? Have a drink before dinner." He took her arm with
his refined, assured manner, his fingers momentarily
pressing into her bare skin.

She felt scorched, a hot lick of excitement against her
ribs. It might have been the first time a man had touched
her. *Slow down,* she thought, shocked by the speed and
intensity of her reactions. This man was *unique.*

A waiter led them to a table in a room lined with
mirrored panels. Huge crystal chandeliers on dimmers
threw a flattering illumination over their heads.

"What will it be?" He looked at her expectantly, his
extraordinary light-filled gaze all the more disturbing for
the fact he cared nothing for his own magnetism. It was
part of him, like the aura that hung over him, the power
and prestige, the great wealth his family had accumu-
lated through successive generations.

"A glass of champagne would be lovely." She turned
her blond head, catching their reflections repeated many
times over in the cross fire of mirrors. They looked like
a study in black and gold.

"Champagne. Why not? We do have something to celebrate." As he spoke to the waiter, Toni found herself studying his profile. His was a bold face in every particular, a face of very definite planes and angles. Not gentle. Strongly sculptured. He had the Beresford cleft chin, not shallow like Joel's, his younger and much more approachable brother, but deeply indented. She thought he would find it a hassle to shave.

"So, have I changed?" He turned swiftly, catching her out.

"Sorry. Was I staring?"

"Just a little."

She shook her head as though to free herself from currents it would be all too easy to plunge into. "I was thinking how familiar your face is to me, yet so unfamiliar. If you can follow my meaning." She broke off.

"Well, we were never contemporaries. You're more of an age with Joel."

"How is he?" she asked.

"Actually, he's thrilled you're coming home."

"Why make it sound like you thought I wouldn't?"

"You haven't bothered before." It came out more harshly than he intended, but she was having the damnedest effect on him. An unwanted rush of desire, under the desire hostility, and deeper yet, a need to put an end to it.

Opposite him, acutely aware of it, Toni's eyes glittered with tears. Her voice fell, as though she was talking to herself. "We'll never be forgiven, will we?"

Those eyes, he thought. Lotus lilies. Blue into violet. "It's done, Toni," he said. "All over with."

There was a pause. "I don't think so, Byrne." She wanted to speak candidly, bridge the gulfs, but there were aspects of Zoe's life she needed to keep private.

"You can't know the difficulties. Zoe was using her maiden name. It complicated things terribly. We were at sea. When we finally got the message, it was too late." She stopped abruptly, anxious not to implicate her mother further. Zoe had an immense capacity for poor judgment. She had kept the news from Toni for days as she battled her own demons.

"Well, it's the nearest you've got to explaining," he said in a terse voice.

Her look of pain was almost physical. "We're still raw with the memory." The whiplash of grief.

The gray eyes assessed, calculated, found her wanting. "Forgive me, Toni, but that's a little hard to believe. Zoe didn't have the slightest difficulty walking out on your father."

"Am I expected to make expiation?" Her nerves tightened powerfully.

"Certainly not to me." His voice was clipped. She was getting too close to him. Under his skin.

"I don't want to have to bear your constant disapproval, Byrne. We are going to be in-laws."

"I wasn't aware I was showing any. You're very lovely, Antoinette." He gave her a glance that left her shaken. "Paris has put a fine polish on you."

"I wasn't talking about my *looks*," she countered a little sadly.

"Good Lord, doesn't everybody?"

Sometimes her looks were a downright disadvantage. Deliberately she changed the subject, picking something safe. "Cate must be very excited."

"She is," he agreed, watching the different expressions chase across her face. "The wedding is having a big impact on all of us. The first wedding on Castle Hill since my grandfather's time. My parents were married in Sydney, as you know.''

"And Dad was best man. I suppose it was inevitable both families would be united at some time. Cate and Kerry have always been great friends. They radiate such warmth and ease when they're together. I suppose it was only natural they would fall in love. They're the lucky ones.''

"Surely you've fallen in love yourself?'' he asked.

"I thought so. Once or twice. It didn't work out.''

"Take your time,'' he advised. "Marriage is a huge risk.''

"Could that be another dig?''

"Not at all,'' he returned. "Clearly you have a chip on your shoulder. How is Zoe?''

She frowned defensively. "She's staying with friends at the moment.''

"Morocco, isn't it?'' Byrne said.

She nodded. "A villa a few miles from the centre of Marrakech. It's very beautiful, a French colonial style farmhouse surrounded by date palms, cedars and lots of silver gray olive trees. Pink bougainvillea smothering the walls.''

"You're really making it sound terribly attractive. You've been there, I take it?''

"Some time ago,'' she acknowledged in a low voice. "Patrick is hoping to marry my mother.''

"No! '' He feigned shock. "Surely that's a little difficult even for Zoe. What does her husband think about it?''

"Shut up, Byrne,'' she said through clenched teeth. Lord, had she said it? She had.

"No, really.'' His smile was cool. "There are a few rules.''

"Mamma hates rules. Besides, Claude is resigned to losing her. He's many years her senior."

"So that makes a difference, does it?" His brilliant eyes were diamond hard.

"It does to Zoe. If a thing doesn't work, it doesn't work."

"Of course, one must be happy at any cost. I assume Patrick's rich?"

The gibe nipped sharply. "Of course, he is. We both know Zoe must have money."

"She appears to have looked after you rather well." His eyes recorded her perfect grooming, the lovely, expensive pink and yellow silk dress.

"I haven't lived off my mother or her husbands," she told him quietly. A point of honour.

"I'm sorry. I understood you followed them all around Europe. You've acquired an accent, by the way. It's utterly charming."

"Would it surprise you if I told you I spoke French like a native?"

"Not at all. So what have you been doing for yourself in Paris?"

His eyes held a cool taunt.

Obviously he wouldn't see her as a dedicated schoolmarm tutoring English, which was what she had been doing quite successfully. That and part-time photographic modelling, mostly featuring her long blond hair.

"I'll tell you some time if you're really interested," she said.

"What's wrong with now?"

"I think you have some preconceived notions about me."

"Actually, Toni, you hadn't established yourself at all." Which wasn't true. She was affecting him strongly.

"After all, your mother spirited you away when you were only seventeen. Kerry missed you terribly. Did you realise that? Especially after your father died."

She heard the little catch in her voice. "It shouldn't have happened."

"No," he agreed, his striking face grim. "Your father grew careless with life. He was profoundly affected by the divorce."

"I loved him, Byrne." She lowered her head, her voice sad.

"He certainly loved you." Adored her, more like it.

"I was devastated when I heard." In fact, she had collapsed, full of hysterical accusations against her mother.

"You couldn't find your way back?" He didn't feel in the least sympathetic, although she made an irresistibly poignant picture.

She gave herself a second to get herself together. "I had serious concerns about Zoe." She couldn't elaborate. "And there was the question of money." At that time she had been pretty well without resources.

"Zoe wouldn't give you any?" One black eyebrow shot up.

"Her nest egg had been more than halved. She was terribly worried. She'd made a disastrous investment. A person she thought highly of abused her trust. Zoe's so *impulsive*. She acts before she thinks."

"Hell, yes," he agreed discordantly, thinking of how hard Eric Streeton had worked for his money. "Let it go, Toni. It's all in the past now."

"Unfortunately the past is never truly past. It follows us around. I was very surprised when Cate wanted me for a bridesmaid."

He knew there had been a big power struggle, the

family dividing into two camps, pro and anti Antoinette. "You got on very well as girls," he said evasively. "You *are* her fiancé's only sister."

"I'm sure that was the only reason I made the bridal party."

"I have to say one or two of us were concerned you mightn't show up on the day." He saw a quick flash of hurt in her eyes and instantly regretted his cutting remark. Lord, was he trying to punish her? Maybe he was.

The waiter returned, bearing a silver tray. He deposited a bottle of Dom Pérignon on the table and proceeded to uncork it, murmuring a fervent thank-you as he pocketed his tip.

"Welcome home," Byrne said, lifting his glass to salute her. "I must apologise, Toni. I'm being too hard on you ."

"I may pay you back one of these days," she retorted, sounding a different person suddenly. "Anyway, you're a hard man."

The gray eyes frosted over. "Is that my reputation, really?"

"Whether you like it or not." She sipped her champagne.

"Listen to me, Toni." He loosened the button of his beautifully cut jacket and eased back. "I've got a lot of people depending on me. A cattle chain to look after. These are tough times. Testing times. Toughness is a quality to be desired. You'd do well to remember it."

"Oh, I will! Be sure of it. And Joel isn't offering a challenge?"

For a moment he looked like he was going to ignore the silky taunt. "I'm not going to put my own brother down, but I think you'll find Joel wouldn't want to take on my responsibilities."

"Just as well, under the circumstances. Personally I don't go along with the old law of primogeniture. Both of you still unmarried?"

He took his time replying, a little nettled, more amused. "Not even engaged. Joel has plenty of time. I'll get around to it when I'm ready."

"You might even have someone already in mind?" She kept those lotus eyes trained on him.

"Not at all."

"You don't need women?" She knew she sounded challenging. But then she'd already been labelled.

"Oh, but I do, Toni. I don't always sleep alone."

No. Indeed not, Toni thought, endeavouring to ignore the shiver that ran down her spine. "Do we name names?"

"No," he said bluntly.

So that was that.

"Drink up and we'll go in to dinner," he murmured. "I've had meetings most of the day. I feel like a Porsche with the engine still running. It will be nice to relax."

Relax they didn't. The tensions tightened a notch, even though an attraction between them was tacitly admitted.

The main dining room was opulent, softly lit, with beautiful paintings and tapestries on the wall, the tables glowing with candles and posies of flowers.

"It's lovely here," Toni murmured appreciatively, watching the light glance off his dark copper skin.

He glanced around, used to grand surroundings from infancy. "The main dining room has recently been refurbished, I understand. If it's all right with you I'd like to get away fairly early in the morning, Toni."

"Have no fear. I won't put you out."

He looked at her keenly, almost laughed. "Well, I'd

like to be at the airport by eight-thirty, at the latest. I suppose it's reasonable to conclude you've brought a fair bit of luggage?''

She grimaced at the implication. "I'm not Mommy Dearest, Byrne. I'm here for the month, then I'll go back to Paris.''

There was a sudden flare in his eyes, like diamonds exposed to bright light. "It sounds like you have someone waiting for you.''

"There is someone.'' She took a deep breath, pretending to go starry eyed.

"There always is.'' He stared at her for a minute before picking up his menu.

"His name is Akbar,'' she confided. "We have crazy times together.''

His handsome mouth tightened. "I'm not sure I'm ready to hear about your little jaunts around Morocco. In many respects I lead a conservative life.''

She opened her eyes wide. "Don't be ashamed of it, Byrne. You're a gorgeous man, really,''

Her power to discomfort him was impressive. "Why, thank you, Antoinette. Just so long as you remember I don't party with youngsters.''

"Which I might say without fear of contradiction lets me out. I'm twenty-two.''

"A considerable age.'' His voice was half mocking, half gentle.

"I'm not going to let you patronise me, Byrne.''

"Good for you. I'm enjoying your efforts.'' He looked at her.

"Oh? I thought you were trying to make me *suffer*.''

That put a brake on him.

"Forgive me, Toni, that wasn't my intention.''

"Of course, I forgive you,'' she lied, anxious to defuse the simmering tension. "As long as you remember something."

"Please don't stop yourself from telling me." He poured them both another glass of champagne.

"I'm not stupid."

He looked at her, light leaping from his silver-gray eyes. "That makes you doubly dangerous."

Toni waited until they were airborne before she allowed herself to speak. "I've got to say I love the new plane." She tapped one beautifully manicured nail against the arm of her chair. "What happened to the Beech Baron?"

"I sold it to Winaroo Downs. It was just what they wanted."

"And this is the Super King Air?"

"Yes. Turbo prop. Averages about two hundred and eighty knots. A jet would have been fairly useless to me, what with trying to find suitable landing strips. This can get in just about anywhere the Baron could, which is what I need. I find I'm doing more flying around the country, checking on other properties, attending meetings, whatever."

"It must have been hellishly expensive," Toni said. Millions. Probably five or six.

"It's not a luxury, Toni, not a rich man's toy. It's a necessity. A way of life. It comfortably seats ten passengers, as well as your seat beside me. A lot of the time I have a full complement on board. Especially when I'm carrying fellow cattlemen. They like to cadge a lift on the most comfortable plane."

"Don't I know." She glanced at the earth. "I never grow tired of flying," she said. "It's a miracle."

"You know Kerry had to part with the Cessna?" He shot her a keen look.

"Of course." She bit her lip. "No matter how hard-working Dad and Kerry were, there were so many reversals."

"And Zoe wanted a big slice of the pie." The old bitterness slipped out.

"I don't know anything about that, Byrne."

"You had to know. Why lie?"

"Dad didn't discuss the settlement with either of us. I was thirteen when Zoe left, remember? Kerry had only just finished school. Dad tried to protect us."

"Then I'm sorry. He wasn't happy about you going off to join your mother, either."

"He agonised, then, loving me, gave in."

"Did she never marry the man she went off with?" Byrne asked after a long pause, "or wasn't he sufficiently well-heeled?"

She looked out the window. Brilliant blue sky and a streaming wedding veil of clouds. "Something like that."

"How long were you with your mother before Von Dantzig disappeared?"

"It was all very distressing, Byrne."

"I bet it was." He felt a sudden wave of protectiveness. "In fact it must have been a nightmare for a beautiful young girl."

"I had nothing to fear. I cried a little when Zoe and Rolf split up. Zoe had already met Claude. He decided to convert her to a grand lady. She liked that."

"Dear, dear." He clicked his tongue. "How did you keep up with these dreadful affairs?"

"I'm infinitely older than my mother," she said simply.

"Is that why you stayed? To protect her?" His eyes were shrewd.

"And all the time you thought I was raging back and forth. Into guys. Into parties. Into drugs." She shot a mocking glance at the hard, handsome profile, which he caught.

"I saw your pals at the hotel."

"What pals?" She blinked in confusion.

"The two who were anxious to get your address."

Her shoulders slumped. "Oh, *them!* You get pleasure seeing me as an air head, don't you?"

"I know perfectly well you're not." She had wit, intelligence, her own apparent strengths.

"Actually I was giving them some tourist destinations on the Barrier Reef. They're Americans, heading that way."

"They didn't invite you?" Hell, he was going out of his way to taunt her.

"All right, they tried. It's no big secret men are convinced blondes know how to enjoy life."

"It sounds just about right to me." He smiled, and it was like the proverbial ray of sunshine spreading radiance across his dark, daunting face.

"Didn't you have a wild girlfriend at one time?" she countered, trying to fight the punch his smile delivered.

"I doubt it, Toni. Wild women aren't my style."

"Yet I seem to remember her. Hettie? Lettie? Tall, good-looking brunette, not shy about spouting off."

"I think you mean Charlotte Reardon." The silver-gray eyes sharpened.

"Yes, Lottie. Everyone said she was very fast."

"What the hell are you up to, Toni?" He raised a brow.

"I just wanted to see if I could take the mickey out of you," she joked.

"You'd better wait until you know me a little better."

"I've known you all my life." Not in this way, she thought. Not with all the flash and challenge.

"Not up close," he told her, eyes narrowing. "Tell me why you really came home."

As a question it was almost aggressive. "To be with Kerry, of course. To be one of Cate's bridesmaids. I consider it an honour."

"What will Zoe do without you?"

"Zoe has made her decision, Byrne. She's going to marry Patrick. There's nothing I can do about it."

"But you've got a problem with it?" He glanced at her, trying to pierce her guard.

"Maybe. Zoe loves weddings. All the excitement and glamour. That wonderful feeling of magic in the air. She doesn't give a lot of thought to *after*."

"Then you can count it a miracle she stayed so long with your father."

"I promise you she did love him," Toni said out of her deep knowledge of her mother. "And there were the two of us."

"A daughter thirteen. A son seventeen. Problematic ages, one would have thought."

"Zoe wasn't qualified to give advice."

He glanced at her with a sympathy he couldn't suppress. "Does she ever show regret?"

Toni rubbed a finger between her arched brows. "One can't judge Zoe by normal standards. She doesn't look on broken marriages as failures. More as a way of breaking out of a bad situation. I should warn you, she could bring Patrick when she arrives."

"So long as she doesn't bring Akbar." Amusement showed in his light-struck eyes.

"All right, I was joking about Akbar."

"Some joke."

"You *believed* me?"

He shrugged. "It must have something to do with the fact you're Zoe's daughter."

"A real flake." That was the general impression *before* they came to know her.

"The sort of woman to drive men wild."

It was difficult suddenly to breathe. "I missed out on *that* talent."

"I've seen nothing to indicate that so far," he drawled. "In fact I'm wondering how we're going to prevent you from upstaging Cate."

Toni flushed with hurt. "That's what I call a bit of out-and-out malice."

"Not at all." His silver eyes sparkled. "Some weddings I've been to the bridesmaid has upstaged the bride."

"That shouldn't happen."

"But it *is* a problem. I suppose you know Cate has three little flower girls lined up, as well as her four bridesmaids?"

Toni smiled. "She always did say she wanted a large wedding. I know Sally and Tara, of course—" she referred to the Beresford cousins "—but I don't think I've met Andrea."

"Andrea Benton."

"Doesn't ring a bell." She looked at him inquiringly.

"You've been out of the country awhile. Andrea's father has been making the news for the past couple of years. Corporate takeovers, that kind of thing."

"It doesn't sound as if you like him."

"I can promise you I like Andrea." He let his gaze skim over her. Thinking, *She doesn't miss a thing*.

"Should I read something significant into that?"

"You're welcome to, if you like." He smiled. "I don't know that it means anything."

"Just a friend of the family?" She shifted position so she could look at him. He was the most marvelous-looking man she had ever seen. Supremely self-assured, and it showed.

"Don't press too hard, Toni," he warned without sounding riled.

"Why, are you scared of matrimony?"

"That's right, ma'am," he drawled.

"Shame on you, Byrne. And you don't like to get yourself into critical situations?"

"You'd better believe it." He took his eyes off the control panel to stare at her. "There are no scandals in the Beresford family."

"None whatsoever?" She couldn't resist it. "Didn't your granduncle have a mistress called Dolly?"

He laughed all of a sudden, and the laughter stayed in his eyes. "Lord, yes, I'd forgotten all about Dolly."

"It's what's called selective memory. But I suppose if we stuck Dolly into the cupboard you'd have been a very worthy family. Maybe a bit starchy." What the heck was she doing, being so irreverent?

"Okay, Antoinette, you've had your little bit of fun."

"Only because you're being pretty mean to me."

He gave her a glance that spangled. "I'm sorry."

She felt a kind of heat spread in her. "Okay, apology accepted. Anyway, I can't talk. I have no immediate plans to get married, either. I'm a bit like you. I'm runnin' scared."

She hoped she might have tweaked his ego, but he laughed. "I guess I asked for that. Was it so bad moving in your mother's circle?" he asked with surprising sympathy.

"Awkward."

"If you needed money to come home, you only had to ask."

"Do you honestly think I'd have approached *you*, Byrne?"

"You had Kerry."

She paused, reflecting. "I don't think Kerry and I will ever get back to what we were."

"That's nonsense!" He gave her a disapproving look. "He loves you."

"He did when we were growing up. But somehow when I wanted to join Zoe he came to believe the Zoe side of me would triumph. It *is* scary the way I look like her. I even talk like her sometimes." She smiled wryly. "Kerry never did identify with Zoe. He's a Streeton through and through. In some ways, too, Kerry left Zoe out in the cold. He was very critical of her and her behaviour from an early age. I think he felt shamed when Zoe flirted with every man in sight. He didn't understand. Flirting is natural to her. She can't stop it. After Zoe divorced Dad, Kerry turned against her completely. I'm not defending Zoe for what she did, but I can see some things from her point of view."

"Of course," he conceded. "I would expect you to be loyal to your mother."

She nodded, dappled sunshine playing over her hair and face. "There is a strong bond between us. The silver cord that can't be severed. There's nothing nasty about Zoe. She might astonish us all with the things she does, but she just *has* to do them. She's like a woman caught in a fantasy world."

"And you're talking about going *back*?" He sounded amazed. "There's nothing more you can do for her, surely? Obviously she gave you no guidance. Do you

need her for all the little extras? I realise neither you nor
Kerry got much out of your father's estate except the
property."

"I can look after myself, Byrne." She pressed her soft
lips together.

"Doing what? You never did tell me."

"I was always in demand tutoring English. I gained
my degree."

He looked at her in quick surprise. "This is the first
I've heard of it."

"You can't know *everything*, Byrne," she said, not
holding back on the sarcasm. "I've worked very hard."

"Well, good for you." His glance was full of approval. "I know you and Kerry did very well at school."

"But you thought I was only enjoying myself?"

"Something like that," he admitted dryly. Hell, they
all had.

"Zoe didn't want me to continue my studies. She
thought, as a woman, I had no need of higher education,
but I made my choice. I wasn't going to bother Zoe with
any demands for money."

His eyes moved sharply to her face. "For the life of
me I can't figure out why. You were entitled. She got
away with enough." In fact, Zoe Streeton had taken her
husband to the cleaners.

"I told you. Zoe made a few bad investments." She
didn't say how bad they really were.

His handsome features tightened, but he remained silent.

"She hasn't a head for business," Toni said defensively. "Kerry didn't write. And when I rang he sounded
very remote."

"That's crazy," he disagreed flatly. "All he wanted
was for you to come home."

"If he did, he never said so." Toni had gotten the strong impression her brother preferred to cope alone. And then he had Cate.

Byrne's scrutiny was intense, cutting through layers of her skin. "I'm not understanding this at all, Toni. Kerry was seriously concerned about you. He was under the impression you and your mother were leading a very giddy life."

Toni shifted in her seat. Kerry hadn't been wrong. It was an empty life Zoe had chosen for herself. A life involving self-indulgence, promiscuity, guile, suffering. A *dreadful* life, Toni thought, but she had tried very hard to protect Zoe and her interests while Zoe went around wondering aloud what was wrong with her daughter. It would have been funny, only the situations Zoe got herself into often landed her in trouble.

"All I can say is, I was there for my mother. What was I supposed to do, abandon her? I can't renounce *my* responsibilities as her daughter. As I see it, it's two-way traffic. She's Kerry's mother, as well, I might point out."

His handsome features were thoughtful. "I should warn you he doesn't want her at the wedding."

"She's coming anyway. It's important to her."

"Is she still as beautiful as ever?" he asked, getting a clear picture of Zoe with the prettiest little girl he had ever seen in her arms.

"Sometimes I think her beauty is indestructible." Toni's smile was soft. "She's forty-seven but she looks thirty-five. She has wonderful skin."

"Which you've inherited." His eyes brushed her, triggering that telltale warmth.

"That part I like."

They were quiet for a while, each seemingly lost in thought. He was such a competent, experienced pilot it was like riding a luxury limousine in the sky. Eventually he spoke. "I'll be putting down on Nowra, as arranged. You'll want time with Kerry to settle in. But we're hoping you'll both come to us for the weekend. My mother thought she'd throw a little party to welcome you back. We'll be having a few houseguests, as well."

"How very kind of her." Toni was a little wary. "But I really don't need a party, Byrne."

"You're darn well going to get it," he drawled. "You'll need to try on your gown. See if it's just right."

"I'm sure it will be lovely."

He gave her a glance that, had she been standing, would have made her legs buckle. "In your case, an understatement. The gowns are in one of the upstairs rooms swathed in muslin, outrageously expensive."

"Bridesmaids usually pay for their own gowns."

"Who would put such a cost on you? No, it's going to be Cate's perfect day, and I'm delighted to make sure it will happen. I'm also delighted she's marrying Kerry. Apart from the fact he loves her so much, our families have always been close. He's a fine young man. Rock solid."

"You're making him sound the least bit dull," Toni protested.

"He is a trifle earnest at the moment. Nothing Cate won't put straight. Kerry's had it hard. He felt his mother betrayed you all. He's missing his father. Both as a parent and Nowra's boss. Kerry's young to take on so much responsibility."

"No younger than you were when your father was killed," she pointed out.

He frowned as if at some remembrance. "My father put me into training at a very early age. I knew what was ahead of me. I knew my obligations. I was mature enough."

"And tough. Unless Kerry has changed a good deal he was never tough. He's more sensitive than anyone knows, except Cate."

"Well, Cate's taking him on now." He smiled at her, a smile that left her shaken. "They'll be together for the rest of their lives. Kerry is now family."

"And he can turn to you when he wants help?" she said quietly.

"I very much hope so. He comes to me now, as it happens."

"I'm sure you'll make a wonderful brother-in-law." Toni couldn't keep the irony from her tone.

"That help applies to you, too."

"I'm not asking for it, Byrne," she said with edgy defiance.

"No, you're not, but it's there all the same."

CHAPTER TWO

THE farther west they flew the more emotional she became. She was home. Really home. She loved Paris with all its wonderful buildings, its bridges, the trees, the restaurants, galleries, museums, the fashion houses, the effortlessly chic women, the charming men, the whole atmosphere that made Paris the most beautiful and evocative city on earth, but this was something else again. Unique.

This was Australia, the great island continent of eight million square kilometres with vast areas of precious wilderness changed little in thousands of years. Here in a land separated for so long from the rest of a war-torn world, peace, freedom and a wonderful sense of the wide-open spaces were inherent in the landscape, in the people. They had passed over sheep country. Now they were heading into the southwest, the fabled home of the cattle kings, descendants of the pioneering fathers, hugely brave and enterprising men who had left their safe, settled homes in the British Isles to make their own fortunes and found their own dynasties.

Like the Beresfords.

It wasn't until after the first World War, in which he had served, that her own great-grandfather took up his huge section. The Beresfords had arrived some sixty years before, every last one of them, despite family tragedies, with the Midas touch. It was the Beresfords who had diversified early, shoring up wealth against the hard times on the land. Where others had gone under despite the fact Australia was the biggest beef exporter in the world, the Beresfords had managed to ride out the storms. Toni knew their portfolio of interests was large. They also did a lucrative trade in polo ponies as the sport gained huge popularity.

Byrne's voice brought her out of her reverie. "How's it going?" he asked, aware of the intensity of her feelings.

She turned her head toward him, her eyes a deep hyacinth. "I love it all so much, the wilderness."

"It's where you were born. It's where you come from. Didn't you ever find even Paris just that bit claustrophobic?"

"On occasions, yes," she admitted. "The noise used to get to me. But the thing I really missed was the smell of the bush, that characteristic scent from all the oils in the leaves and the stems of the eucalypts. I even burned a pile of eucalypt leaves once so I could inhale the fragrance of home."

He glanced at her. "Hard to believe then you're going back to Europe."

"Zoe is expecting me. She relies on me for lots of things." She looked at her linked hands.

"What is she, a child?"

The answer to that was yes. "What is there for me here?" she countered. "I may have a half share in Nowra, but I can't *live* there. Cate will be mistress of Nowra."

"Which puts you in an unfair position," he commented. "The station wouldn't be returning all that much at this time. You've never approached Kerry for your share?"

"Good Lord, no. Nowra is Kerry's life. He loves it

with a passion. How could I possibly ask him to sell out our heritage?''

"He couldn't do it *now*," Byrne warned. "But it *could* be done.''

"Despite your earlier offer, I can't accept any help from you, Byrne," she said swiftly.

"You could have softened that a little.''

"*You* don't pull any punches.''

"Perhaps not. But what I meant was, and this could be discussed with Kerry, he could take out a loan.''

"And you'd be guarantor?''

"It's an idea.''

"Certainly. It's also quite possible you want me out of Nowra altogether.''

He swung his handsome head. "Hang on, now," he said crisply. "I was thinking of *you*.''

She thought about it a moment, reasoned it could be true. "Then I apologise. But the issue has to be faced. Nowra will be Kerry's and Cate's home. They'll have an heir who will want to continue the family tradition. The fact I own half of Nowra complicates matters.''

"It does a little," he conceded.

"So it's just as I thought.''

"Have it your own way, Toni. You will. I can see it in your eyes.''

There was a brisk crosswind blowing when they touched down at Nowra. Despite that, they made a text-book landing. Kerry was waiting for them outside the silver hangar, waving at them, looking so utterly dear, Toni burst into tears.

"So you've missed him more than you think?" Byrne murmured, touched by her lovely tear-tracked face.

"Of course I have." Her voice was shaky as she

fought to level it. "This is my brother. My dearest friend."

He saw it in her eyes.

As soon as her feet touched the ground Kerry was there, throwing out his arms, swinging her off her feet and hugging her tight. "Toni, Toni, it's so good to see you." He held her away from him. "You've grown even more beautiful."

"So have you," she said, and laughed shakily. "You're so much like Dad. It's wonderful to be home. To see you at long last. I've missed you terribly."

"Then that makes two of us, poppet." He used his childhood name for her, holding her around the waist while he turned to Byrne. "Thanks so much, Byrne, for bringing Toni home. I'm very grateful."

Byrne shrugged it off. "It's been a pleasure. I enjoyed it."

Toni turned a radiant face to him, catching a long windblown skein of hair. "You'll stay and have a cup of coffee, won't you, Byrne?"

"I'd like to," he said lightly, surprising himself by gently brushing the skein from her damp cheeks, "but I have a client flying in this afternoon. He wants to pick out a couple of polo ponies."

"Well, he's dealing with the best," Kerry affirmed. "Everything set for the weekend?" He glanced from one to the other.

"Sure." Byrne was relaxed. "I've spoken to Toni. There should be about twenty people in all, excluding family, which means you two. Nothing Toni can't handle. She's amazingly poised and chic."

"She looks like one of those super models. The blonde," Kerry said with a grin, his eyes moving over his sister's slender figure. She was wearing a summery pink shirt and hipster pink jeans with a very fancy belt, and she looked terrific. "And she's gone and got herself an accent. I don't know how that's going to go down with the locals."

"A few weeks home and it'll flatten out," Toni promised. "I'll call your mother to thank her, Byrne."

He nodded, inclined his dark head. "She'll be pleased."

Toni wasn't remotely fooled by that. Sonia Beresford had never approved of Zoe. Indeed, she had on several occasions yielded to the temptation to say so. Toni was uncomfortably aware most people believed she had followed in her mother's footsteps. A case of blurred identity. Unfair, but a fact. She had her whole life in front of her. She intended to make a success of it, not leave a lot of damaged people in her wake.

They had afternoon tea on the wide, cool veranda that looked out on the infinite rolling plains. Station horses grazed in a home paddock, a brilliant sun flashed off distant windmills, and a wedge-tail eagle soared buoyantly over the house, its great wings outstretched. It was almost like she had never been away. Nowra homestead wasn't a grand colonial mansion like the Beresfords' Castle Hill, but it was a very agreeable house indeed, with an English formality in the layout of the rooms. Two-storeyed, it was built of local stone bleached a lovely soft cream from the sun. The shutters on the top storey, the French doors on the veranda, the wooden bracketing valances and the railings were painted a pristine white. It was charming, the long three-mile drive lined with wonderful towering gums. The interior, however, was desperately in need of refurbishing. For all her skills at twisting their father around her little finger, Zoe had never been able to do much to change the decoration, essentially unchanged from their great-grandfather's day. The heaviness, the dimness and the massive pieces of Victorian furniture remained. Toni would have dearly loved to do the refurbishing herself. She had come to realise she had a fine hand with decorating, but that was out of the question. Although she had an equal share in Nowra Station, it would be Cate's home, and Cate would be a great deal more successful in effecting alterations than Zoe had been. Moreover, Cate came with a huge dowry, a definite asset if one wanted to transform what by today's standards was a very large house.

What exactly is mine? Toni wondered, mulling over her conversation with Byrne. The station was only breaking even. There was little ready cash. Unlike Cate, she wasn't an heiress, though her share of Nowra if she sold out would make her secure.

"You look so serious, poppet. What are you thinking about?" Kerry folded his hands behind his head.

Toni smiled, her face soft with affection. "I'm thinking it feels like I've never been away."

He glanced across the garden, stripped back to low maintenance. "Why did you never come home, Toni?" he asked, old suffering in his eyes. "I've asked myself that question every day. I missed you so much. It was terrible without Dad. He needn't have died. Septicemia. God! I told him about that gash, but he didn't seem to think it was serious. Byrne got him into hospital. Flew him there himself, but Dad's resistance was low—" He broke off, distressed. A tall, handsome young man, an all-over golden brown—hair, eyes, skin.

"*Don't*, Kerry," she begged. "I know how it was."

"You *can't*, Toni. You weren't here."

"For which I'll always mourn. I was a victim of cir-

cumstance. So was Zoe. We never wanted the terrible
mix-ups to happen.''

"Then why did she drop the name Streeton, for God's
sake?'' he asked.

Toni closed her eyes, trying to contain an unwarranted
sense of guilt. "It was all meant to be, Kerry.'' She
sighed fatalistically. "Zoe had started a new life. She's
into playacting. You know that. When the police finally
worked out exactly *who* she was and *where*, it was all
too late. She was shocked out of her mind. Overcome
by remorse. She couldn't even get her courage up to tell
me for days. The funeral was over. She reasoned there
was nothing we could do.''

"God!'' Kerry rose abruptly and went to the balus-
trade, staring into infinity. "Isn't that typical Zoe. She
never could make the right decision.''

"She tries hard to, Kerry, but she never learned how.''

"You should have come home.''

"I'm so sorry,'' Toni answered quietly.

"There's more to this, isn't there?'' He turned to con-
front her. "You're always protecting Zoe. You did when
you were only a little girl and someone said something
about her. She doesn't deserve all this devotion, Toni.''

"Yes, she does.'' Toni felt her eyes sting with tears.
"She's my *mother*. She's a child. She'll never be finished with growing up. For a time she went off the deep
end. She was distraught. It was almost as though she had
killed Dad herself.''

"Well, didn't she?'' Kerry nearly choked with tears.

"She didn't understand that, Kerry, when she walked
out on him.''

"*Us.*''

"I know it's hard. Zoe didn't love any of us in the
way we wanted. It's a fact of life, and it has to be ac-

cepted. On the other hand, she can't bear to be on her own. She told me she'd kill herself if I went off and left her.''

Kerry stared at her, looking incredulous. ''Zoe wouldn't kill herself for anything. Unless she lost her looks or her money. *Our* money. She bled Dad dry. Fancy getting paid for adultery.''

Toni went pale at his deep core of anger.

''Did you believe she was serious?'' Kerry asked.

''It wasn't any suicide trial, Kerry. She landed herself in the hospital. A couple more pills would have swung it.''

For moments he didn't answer. Then with a haunted look, Kerry crossed to his sister, went down on his haunches, held her hand. ''Why didn't you tell me?''

''Defending Zoe is a habit,'' she said simply. ''It was a side of Zoe I didn't want you to know about. She's like a snappy little sports car without a brake. *I* was the brake.''

''That I believe.'' Kerry's voice was thin and strained. ''It would have upset me, too. I hope I don't have a child like that. It must be in our genes.''

''I pray Zoe is a one-off,'' Toni answered soberly. ''I know I attract a lot of flack because of her. From your prospective brother-in-law, for one.''

''Byrne?'' Kerry's eyebrows shot up. ''I wouldn't think Byrne would want to hurt you or give you a bad time. He's not like that.''

''He doesn't think much of Zoe,'' she said wryly.

''No one thinks much of Zoe, poppet, and that's a sad fact. I was so worried she'd try to change you. Turn you into some frivolous doll. I remember how she always wanted to dress you like one, and you hated it. When you didn't come back, we all thought she'd won you over. You were only a kid when you left.''

''I grew up quick.'' Toni looked back on the years with a kind of disbelief.

''Is she really coming home for the wedding or was that a lot of hot air?'' Kerry asked.

''In as much as anyone can count on Zoe, the answer's yes.''

''You haven't fallen in love yet?''

''One mildly passionate affair.''

''So what happened?''

''He got too possessive. I don't like that. Besides, I'm not ready to settle down for a long, long time. When I marry I want it to be forever. Like you and Cate. I'm so thrilled for you, Kerry. It must be wonderful to meet that one special person who makes up your other half.''

''That's the way it's always been with us,'' Kerry said, a deep contentment in his voice. ''I've always loved Cate. Even when we were kids. She feels the same way about me. We've always been sure of our feelings.''

''Lucky you.'' Toni felt a lump in her throat. ''And it's going to be a great big wedding.''

''The wedding of the year.'' He smiled. ''It's not every day a Beresford marries.''

''And a Streeton. Don't let's forget that,'' she said briskly.

''You're going to make a gorgeous bridesmaid.'' Kerry spoke with pride. ''In fact, you're going to put Andrea Benton's nose out of joint.''

''Why's that?'' Toni felt uneasy.

''Don't you know?''

''Nope.''

''She's got her sights set on Byrne.'' Kerry put his cup down and leaned forward confidentially.

"Really? She's a brave woman, indeed, to set her sights so high."

"Mad about him," Kerry told her, nodding owlishly.

"I thought every woman around was mad about him."

"True, but then Byrne has very exacting standards."

"Of course. I'm not that stupid I forgot."

"Had quite a crush on him one time, didn't you?" Kerry teased.

"You speak one word about it and I'll kill you," Toni threatened, spoiling it with a sweet, easy smile.

"My lips are sealed," Kerry said in a cheery voice. "I wish you'd stay, Toni."

Toni hesitated, shook her head. "Impossible, kiddo. Two's company, three's a crowd."

"I *need* you," he said quietly. "I love Catherine, but I need my sister, too. My own blood."

"Understandable." She felt warmed. "We don't really have anyone, do we? The Beresfords have a whole army of relatives."

"Which reminds me. Joel's quite mad to see you again."

"Good Lord, why?" Toni was disconcerted.

"You can't be serious?" Kerry stared at her, trying not to laugh. Toni never did have any vanity about her looks. Neither did their mother, for that matter.

"Indeed I am. Joel was only a kid when I left. We always got on, but there was no great rapport, like you and Cate."

"The thing is, you're all grown up now. So's he."

"This has nothing to do with matchmaking, has it?" she challenged him, astonished.

Kerry thought. "Something has to keep you home," he said finally.

Toni looked at her brother directly, holding his eyes. "I'm not ready for marriage, Kerry. Much less to a Beresford."

"What's that supposed to mean?"

"I wouldn't care to have to dance to Byrne's tune," she said, with a slight flush. "He has a lot of power and influence over his entire family."

"So? He's the best guy in the world, Toni. I know he can be pretty formidable at times. Believe me, he has to be, but you couldn't ask for a better friend and supporter."

Toni shook her head ruefully. "You haven't had to ask him for money, have you? I know times have been tough."

Kerry sighed. "Mostly he gives advice. I have Jock, Drew and the boys to help me. They're good cattlemen, and they've been with us forever, but they don't have Byrne's experience or business expertise."

"So he *did* loan you money?"

"He's helped out, yes."

"To the tune of what?"

"A hundred thousand or so," Kerry said, as casually as he could. "A drop in the ocean, really. He'll get it back. Unlike us, the Beresfords don't rely solely on the beef chain. They're into everything. Byrne's positively brilliant when it comes to making money. He's way ahead of the field."

"I daresay, and it's not at all unusual. They seem to pass the talent along, but it puts us under an obligation to him, doesn't it?"

"Toni, you heard him yourself. We're family."

"*You're* family. I'm not. I've been given the role of outsider. I suppose, as you're getting married, we should talk about our affairs," she said simply.

"You don't want me to pay you out, do you, Toni?" Kerry looked worried. "I understand the funny position you're in, but right now it's out of the question."

"No, that's not it at all." Toni shook her head. "But I'm thinking the Beresfords have a way of taking over. Byrne has already touched on the subject."

"In what way?" The look of anxiety remained in Kerry's eyes.

"Maybe you'd prefer to discuss it with him yourself. He suggested it, as a matter of fact."

"No. You tell me."

Toni studied her brother's face. "He was thinking it might be possible for you to get a loan."

Kerry reacted swiftly. "Not the kind of money you're entitled to. Not unless I had—"

"A guarantor?"

"Aha!" Kerry looked at his strong hands.

"Byrne would want his sister to be sole mistress of Nowra. You do see that?"

Kerry shifted in his chair. "Cate's never said anything."

"I imagine she has plans to refurbish the house," Toni said reasonably.

"I'm not marrying her for her money." Kerry brushed back his thick curly hair.

"Good Lord, you don't have to tell *me* that. I'm only saying that Cate is a very confident person. She's coming from a very secure place. She'll want to run her own home."

"I do know she wants to make certain changes," Kerry admitted.

"That's okay by me. It could only be for the better. I know you like familiar things around you, Kerry—you're a lot like Dad—but the house will be lovely light-

ened up. I never did go along with all the Victoriana.
Neither did Zoe.''

"She couldn't change Dad there," Kerry said almost
with satisfaction.

"I hope you're not thinking of putting a brake on
Cate," Toni warned.

"She wouldn't let me." He looked at her and grinned.
"I make no bones about it. Cate's the boss."

Which was probably true, Toni thought. Cate was a
strong, positive individual who liked to take charge. It
was part of her attraction for Kerry. As he turned away
from his mother, he reached out for a strong female figure. One who valued hard work, loyalty, love. Cate was
a mother figure in a disguised form. Even as a girl she
had been a very capable person, springing instantly to
Kerry's defense on any occasion even if he was only
mildly under attack. There were four years between her
and her brother. She and Cate had never been close, but
there had never been the slightest friction between them.
Cate had asked her to be her chief bridesmaid, but Toni
had the feeling Sonia Beresford wouldn't have wanted
to go along with that idea. Probably not Byrne, either.
He had all but told her her defection to Zoe had reduced
her standing in everyone's eyes.

Byrne picked them up in the Castle Hill helicopter at
nine-thirty sharp Saturday morning. Kerry was all smiles
at the prospect of spending the weekend with his beloved, but Toni, despite her varied and sometimes downright distressing experiences over the past years, felt a
flutter of nerves. Arriving at Castle Hill wasn't exactly
like flying into the lion's den, but she couldn't help feeling she'd be under the microscope. A polo match, a final

between amateur teams from all over the Outback, was due to start at three.

"Two matches even," Kerry told her, a proud member of Byrne's team, which comprised the two Beresford brothers, Kerry and Sandy Donaldson, a big-shot player from Emu Downs, a sheep and cattle property in Central Queensland.

"It'll be a great game, Toni," Kerry promised. "Plenty of drama with Byrne on the field."

"Just so long as you don't come a cropper." Byrne gave him a lazy smile. "You have to walk down the aisle in a month's time."

"I know how to hold my own." Kerry grinned. "You're the player. Hell, you won our first match at a canter."

"The supreme man's man!" Toni widened her eyes in mock admiration.

Once they were airborne, Toni saw the infinite blue sky without a single speck of cloud stretched from horizon to horizon. She felt her heart racing as she looked. Castle Hill was the flagship of the Beresford chain. It had been built up and enlarged with steely determination from generation to generation, its history a larger-than-life saga that really needed recording. It was full of high drama, of danger and tragedy, of drought and flood and one terrible fire in the early 1920s when an entire wing of the homestead had been destroyed and a Beresford son had lost his life. The station took its name from a monolithic sandstone hill that towered behind the homestead and that resembled an ancient ruined castle. There were many of these extraordinary castle-like formations scattered throughout the Outback, but Castle Hill, or Korrunda Koorun, as the aborigines called it, was one of the most spectacular. Over the years Toni had seen it

in all its manifestations. Glowing fiercely against the cobalt sky, larkspur at dawn and at dusk, impossible to
describe at sunset when it flashed gold and rose, ominous
when the great electrical storms blew and it glinted silver, lurid green and black. The aborigines looked on
Korrunda Koorun as a sacred site, spirit-haunted, not
fantasy but closely associated with many a scary tale
family and staff kept locked away in their hearts. Usually
Castle Hill was benign, a truly wonderful natural feature
to be admired, but all of them had felt its occasional
menace.

Today it looked spectacular, standing like a great for-
tress with the homestead at its feet. Byrne landed them
on the front lawn of the grand colonial set so incongru-
ously in a million wild acres, but for all the grandness
of the mansion, it was the unique setting that filled the
visitor with the greatest shock of excitement.

"That's not your hand trembling, is it?" Byrne asked
as he helped her descend onto the ground.

"Don't tease." Nervous, she forced herself to speak
lightly.

"What are you afraid of?" His vibrant voice was surprisingly gentle.

"You might eat me for dinner."

"I'd be more interested in kissing you."

That brought her head up. She stared at him, finding
lights flickering in his brilliant eyes. "Don't endanger
yourself doing it," she warned.

"I can take care of myself, Antoinette." He brought
his gaze deliberately to her soft, luscious mouth.

"Ah, the optimism of the confirmed bachelor." Toni
was grateful the breeze was cooling her cheeks.

"Really. I can get married any time I like."

"Lord knows, you're entitled," she managed to say,

smooth as honey. "I almost feel sorry I'm not available."

"I'm not a baby snatcher, either."

"Byrne Beresford, I'm way over the legal age." Her violet eyes glowed.

He brought up his hand and mussed her shining hair a little. "To me you're a *minor*."

"Could it be you feel threatened?" Suddenly she was enjoying herself, caught between the need for control and going off like a rocket.

"Distracted, maybe." Byrne's silver eyes sparkled like coins in the sunlight.

"Well, I figure that's good enough."

He threw a glance over her shoulder, and Toni turned. Two women were coming down the steps, the older with some regality as befitted the mistress of Castle Hill, the younger, tall, slim, dark-haired, at an excited rush.

"Front up, young Streeton," Byrne drawled.

Cate went into her fiancé's waiting arms, turning to beam radiantly at his sister. "Toni, how lovely to see you. You've grown every bit as beautiful as Byrne said. Welcome home."

Toni moved spontaneously so they could exchange a kiss. "I'm thrilled to be home, Cate. Thank you so much for wanting me as your bridesmaid. I'm honoured."

"How could I *not* have you?" Cate exclaimed. "We'll be sisters in a month's time. I've always wanted a sister."

"Antoinette, my dear." Sonia Beresford had reached them, a handsome, forceful woman of well above average height with dark gray eyes, a thick sweep of near black hair and a manner that suggested she never, but never lost her cool.

"Mrs. Beresford."

Toni was hugged lightly. "Welcome home, my dear. I hope you're not going to go off and leave us again?"

"My plans are a little unsettled at the moment, Mrs. Beresford," Toni said, keeping her mouth curved in a smile. "I'm so thrilled and excited about the wedding."

"We all are, my dear. Our two families united." Sonia Beresford looked with pride at her son, then turned her patrician head to Kerry. "And how are you, my dear?"

"Fine, Sonia." A white smile lit Kerry's attractive face. "It's wonderful having Toni back. We talked into the small hours and we still haven't talked ourselves out."

"So much to catch up on, dear."

"Take the bags to the veranda, would you, Pike?" Byrne spoke to an approaching houseman. Giving orders was a Beresford way of life, Toni thought.

"Well, don't let's stand here in the hot sun. Come into the house," Sonia said in her smooth contralto.

"I'll catch up with you later," Byrne said, sketching a brief salute.

"You'll be back in time for lunch, won't you, darling?" his mother asked a little anxiously.

"Sure. I wouldn't miss it for the world," he answered, and gave Toni a final sizzling glance.

"Notice any changes?" Sonia asked as they walked to the house.

"It looks perfect, as always," Toni said. "That magnificent white creeper is new." She looked toward the lofty exterior of the two-storeyed building, a central core flanked by two large wings set to form a semicircle. The stone pillars of the ground floor formed a magnificent colonnade that was festooned with a luxuriant creeper bearing masses of pure white trumpet flowers.

"I got very tired of the bougainvillea," Sonia explained. "It made a wonderful display but it was hard to control. The moonflower has been in for about three years. It's just perfect for the wedding. It flowers right through spring and summer."

Inside the house Toni could see at a glance it had been refurbished on the grand scale for the coming wedding. Her partial view of the drawing room revealed the walls had been hung with a beautiful new paper in glowing yellow that went splendidly with the gold frames of the mirrors and paintings and the gold cornices that set off the white-plastered ceiling and the gold and white bookcases. It looked lovely and light and airy, yellow taffeta curtains at the long line of French doors.

Sonia caught her looking. "Plenty of time to go over the house, dear. It needed a little decorating, and now was the perfect time to do it. Let me show you to your room. You'll want to settle in."

They walked up the spectacular central staircase, possibly the most striking feature of the house, to the landing that divided to lead to the upper floor and the richly adorned gallery flooded with light from the glass dome above. The suite of bedrooms was off the gallery, and Sonia gestured toward the west wing. Like the entrance hall and the drawing room, the gallery had been repainted, its elaborate plasterwork continuing the yellow, white and gold theme. It looked remarkably beautiful and graceful, and it would have cost the earth.

Sonia waved a vaguely apologetic hand.

"Even Byrne had to question all the money that was being spent. But it's not every day one's only daughter gets married. And from home. I'm so thrilled about that. You're down this way, my dear. You'll have a lovely view of the walled garden."

Sonia paused outside an open doorway and stood back for Toni to precede her. The room was lovely, decorated in French pieces, including the antique bed, the colour scheme pink and white. She had never in her life stayed at the homestead, although her parents had on many occasions for balls, parties and the like.

"Like it?" Sonia smiled at Toni's transparent expression.

"It's a beautiful room, Mrs. Beresford. Enchanting."

"And it's yours for the wedding." Sonia walked to an arrangement of pink roses on the small writing desk and tweaked at a stray flower. "Really, I had a marvellous time doing everything up. I can only hope when Byrne makes his mother happy and chooses a bride she shares my tastes."

"I love everything I've seen." Toni smiled, walking to the open French doors and looking over the walled section of the garden. "You're a wonderful gardener, as well."

"These days, dear, I only do the planning," Sonia said. "I don't like to talk about it, but I've developed arthritis in my hands. Just like my dear mother. I'm not having the lawns mown until the day before the wedding. I want them to stay green. We use bore water, of course, and we were very fortunate with the winter rains. A miracle, really, after so many daunting years. The long-range forecast is for heavy rain over tropical Queensland about Christmas, so we'll eventually get the floodwaters."

"And the wildflowers," Toni said. "Some of my friends in Paris didn't believe me when I told them the desert blooms like the Garden of Eden after rain. I don't think, either, they could appreciate the sheer size of the country or the vast wilderness areas."

"We try to keep it our secret." Sonia smiled. "So how was life in Paris, my dear?" Her gray eyes settled on Toni's graceful figure as she began to walk from bedroom to dressing room to hang up the few garments she had brought with her. Sonia spotted something eye-catching covered in plastic. For the party, she guessed correctly.

"Wonderfully stimulating," Toni said. "Paris is everything it's claimed to be. You'd know, you've been there often. But it's great to be home."

"Byrne tells me you managed to fit in a degree."

"Yes, in the arts. I always did enjoy study, learning new things."

"I remember that now. Kerry was an excellent student, as well. He's a fine young man. We're delighted to welcome him into the family."

Although it was said warmly, Toni got the faintest impression Sonia Beresford might have been better pleased had her only daughter aimed higher.

"You know you've acquired an accent?"

"So everyone tells me. It's hard not to."

"But it's charming. You've also acquired a great deal of poise," Sonia said with approval. She thought Toni wore her clothes extremely well, a plum silk shirt with sand-coloured linen pants, yet the grace of her body made the outfit enormously chic.

"I think Paris would have to be one of the great finishing schools in the world," Toni said. "I learned a lot just observing."

"And how is your mother?" Sonia asked smoothly. "Keeping well, I hope?"

"I don't think Zoe's ever had a sick day in her life." If one discounted that stomach-churning suicide attempt, Toni thought.

"Is she still as beautiful?" Sonia asked with a faint note of envy.

"My mother's a very fortunate woman. Her beauty is unimpaired."

"Do you really think she'll return for the wedding, Toni?"

Toni was quiet for a moment. "She says she's going to, Mrs. Beresford."

"Oh, *Sonia,* please." The older woman waved an imperious hand. "We're going to be family now, Toni. We can afford to discard the formalities."

Toni inclined her head in acknowledgment. "Zoe is delighted Cate and Kerry are to be married, Sonia. She's always admired the family and she's always had a soft spot for Cate. Whether she actually makes it home is a little hard to say. She says she's coming."

Sonia's well-shaped mouth was compressed. "All's well with her marriage?"

Toni turned from the chest of drawers. "Didn't Byrne tell you?" Of course he had. "She's contemplating leaving Claude."

Sonia's face set wryly. "She doesn't do things by halves, does she?"

"No." Toni shook her head.

"You know Kerry doesn't want her here?"

Toni felt a sigh run through her. "He told me. How does Cate feel?"

"You know Cate, my dear." Sonia shrugged. "She sides with Kerry in everything. But she certainly won't say anything to you. She knows how close you are to your mother."

"So far as I can see I'm her only real friend."

"And I admire you for it, Antoinette," Sonia responded, a brief glint in her eyes. "Family loyalty is important."

"I'm looking forward to seeing Sally and Tara again," Toni said, to ease the strain.

"And they you," Sonia fibbed, remembering how both women had been very much against Cate's choice of her chief bridesmaid. "You haven't met Andrea. She's due in at noon. Just in time to join us for lunch. She's a very attractive young woman. Well educated, well travelled. She's very taken with Byrne, but I don't really know how he feels about her. He's obviously in no hurry to get to the altar. Once I used to think there wasn't a woman good enough for him. Now I can't wait to see him married with a family. He'll be thirty-two next birthday. Time to produce grandchildren and Castle Hill's heir." She loved all her children, but she worshipped her firstborn.

"And Joel?"

Sonia laughed. "I've lost track of Joel's romances. He's never serious for long, though I'm honor bound to tell you he's very keen to see you. Especially when Byrne said you were ravishing."

"That was nice of Byrne."

"A plain statement of fact," Sonia answered dryly, foreseeing her nieces' reaction. "By the way, dear, you'll have to try on your bridesmaid dress. I know you sent us your measurements but there might be some slight alteration necessary. We've matched the colours of the gowns to your colouring and the colours in the bridal sheaf Cate will be carrying. She doesn't want a bouquet and she's tall enough to carry off a sheaf. Sally will be wearing peony pink, Tara a lovely lilac, Andrea a leaf green to match her eyes and you violet. The fabric is duchesse silk satin, as you know, strapless as is all the rage, with little off-the-shoulder guipure boleros fitting just under the bust for the ceremony. You can take them off later if you want. The bridal sheaf colours will be picked up in the bridesmaids' headdresses.''

"Sounds lovely."

Sonia smiled with deep satisfaction. "Gorgeous. The little ones are to wear magnolia taffeta with a tulle underskirt and different sashes to match the bridesmaids. The same goes for the men's vests. Cate's gown is absolutely beautiful. She looks marvellous in it. I'll let her show it to you herself. Now I must be off. Lots of things to do. We'll meet up again at lunch. Then there's polo this afternoon and our little party tonight."

"Thank you once again for giving it for me, Sonia. It's very kind."

"A pleasure, my dear." Sonia Beresford walked to the door and paused. "You know, despite your extraordinary resemblance to Zoe, you have a decided look of your father. Something about the expression and the way you turn your head. You're not Zoe's build, either. No, there are glimpses of Eric there."

Maybe enough to save me, Toni thought.

CHAPTER THREE

THE canyon was long and narrow, with steep walls that blazed like wildfire. At regular intervals they had to ford a stream, shallow now but a rampaging torrent when fed by the northern monsoons. Slender ghost gums flourished on both sides of the rugged escarpment, their white limbs highlighting a brilliant blue sky. He and two of his men had been tracking "clean skins" since dawn, unbranded cattle that sought to evade the muster by hiding out in the canyon with its water and great variety of vegetation. They were gaining on the mob steadily. When they finally caught up he would return to the house. He didn't want to be away any longer than was necessary. He had the polo match scheduled for the afternoon, which rather surprisingly was taking a back seat in his mind to the arrival of Miss Antoinette Streeton. For the first time in a long time he felt a quickening of flesh and blood. It gave him a certain ironic enjoyment. He was beginning to think the only thing he could revel in was his love for the land. *His* land. Castle Hill. Now, totally out of the blue, young Toni Streeton with her Parisian gloss. It was a physical thing, of course. He derived an intense pleasure from beauty in any form. No, be fair. From her radiant presence. She was so much Woman, that mysterious goddess-like creature who held men spellbound. It was all very stimulating. But it couldn't go anywhere. More than anything he wanted to preserve his perfect wholeness, the sense of being his own master.

A kilometer along the canyon a large red kangaroo suddenly jumped from a high point on the escarpment onto the white pebbled floor, startling the horses, who reared wildly in protest at the kangaroo's senseless antics. Samson, his aboriginal tracker, so called because of his long, luxuriant black hair and full beard, swore colourfully as he reined his horse in, then, when the animal quieted, leaned over to gently pat its side. There were more kangaroos farther down, a half dozen big reds drinking lazily at a pool coloured a lime green, but they bounded away as the riders galloped toward them. They were in clear sight of the mob now, driving them out of the canyon at a hectic rush, whips cracking harmlessly over their backs.

As they broke out onto the grasslands Beresford turned his horse away and called a final instruction. It would take a good half hour's ride to reach the main compound. The whole exercise had taken a little longer than he had anticipated. He pulled his Akubra over his eyes and put the big gelding to the gallop, causing great clouds of emerald to rise from the graceful willowy canopy of desert oak. Budgerigar. They scattered like so much confetti thrown at a wedding. It was a sight he saw every day of his life, yet he was still touched by the magic.

By the time he reached the main compound he was pretty much played out. A nice cold shower would revive him. He felt hot and disheveled, his face and denim shirt sheened with fine red dust and splotches of muddy water he had picked up in the chase. At the stables he threw the reins to one of the boys who came running, swept off his Akubra and wiped the sweat from his brow. He could enter the house from the rear, using the utility room that formed part of the kitchen complex to wash the worst of the dust from his face and hands.

Inside the house he heard the voice of their longtime housekeeper, Bridie, who reigned supreme over the household staff. As usual she was giving instructions to her helpers, young aboriginal girls from the mission who chose to live and work on the station to be close to their roots. It worked very well. The girls were as cheerful as they were efficient, and they took the load off Bridie, who was now in her sixties.

He laughed when he saw his face in the mirror above the washbasin. He looked like a bush ranger, a dangerous man on the run. His hair, released from the wide-brimmed hat, sprang into a mad tousle of crow-black waves he never could iron out, the grime accentuating the peculiar glitter of his eyes. Hell, even he thought they were strange eyes. The eyes of a fanatic, a visionary? He was no saint. A quick wash restored him to something like normality. He flung the used towel into a basket and strode out of the room, through the lobby, past the wall of pantries and the large refrigerated room to the staircase that would take him to his suite of rooms in the east wing.

One hand on the newel, his foot on the first stair, a ribbon of sound stopped him. Light humming, interspersed with a few sweet melodious notes. A woman's voice. It was coming from the old ballroom, a vast room in the centre of the house accessed from the entrance hall. The last time it had been used was for Cate's twenty-first birthday. Now it would be the scene for her wedding ceremony, with the overflow of guests spilling into the library that adjoined it.

His next movement was completely involuntary. Another thing that astounded him. He found himself treading softly down the passageway, keeping to the Persian runner to muffle the sound of his riding boots. He reached the open double doorway of the ballroom and glanced inside.

A young woman danced alone to a slow melody, her eyes half closed, her arms positioned as though she was in the arms of an imaginary partner. One she was in love with. Her expression was dreamy, her mouth curved in a blissful soft smile. She was wearing a summery white dress, extraordinarily incandescent in that dark-panelled room with the incoming light pouring through the soaring casements. The skirt of her dress, clinging lightly to her hips, flared as she moved. The long silver gilt hair moved, too, fanning out in a way that made him want to catch hold of it, bury his face in it, run his fingers through the silky scented length.

Lord, what was wrong with him? He was no callow boy, yet he couldn't take his eyes off her. It was almost as though he had been rendered powerless. He could only stand and stare, watching her enchanted performance. She was as beautiful as a painting, moving into a ray of light that clung to her like some heavenly nimbus. Her footsteps on the golden polished floor with its handsome border were almost soundless. She might have been a lovely apparition, an angel come to visit.

He felt the odd conflict stir in him again. Being powerless didn't suit him. Besides, it was the last thing he needed or wanted.

He brought his hands together in a slow burst of applause. "Maybe tonight we can find you a partner?" Even to his own ears his voice sounded mocking.

She stopped immediately, turning to face him. No trace of embarrassment. "Byrne, you startled me." The violet eyes sparkled with stars.

"You were that far away?" Again he was compelled to move closer, though he felt moody and disturbed.

"I haven't danced like that for ages!" She gave a breathless laugh. "Wherever we've been it has always been so crowded. Are you thinking of having dancing here tonight?"

"Why not?" he responded, his eyes on her lovely face. "We might as well get as much use out of the room as we can. You know the reception will be held in the old stone stables complex?"

"So Kerry told me. You've had it specially renovated."

He nodded. "It has historic significance for us and a great deal more atmosphere than the main hall. In fact, I have to say it warrants all the money that has been spent on it. Cate will be sure to want to show you over it. Probably tomorrow. There's so much going on today." Abruptly he awoke to the fact he must still look like a wild man. "You'll have to excuse how I look," he said wryly. "I've been clearing out clean skins most of the morning. I was on my way to take a shower when I heard you."

"How did you know it was me?"

"The siren call." His tone was dry but his eyes were intense.

"Is that how you think of it?"

"Let's say once you hear it you've no choice but to follow."

"I hope that means you're going to dance with me tonight?"

"I'm a terrible dancer." His lean, powerful body had a touch of tension.

"You couldn't be. Not the way you move. Why don't

you let me be the judge?'' Impishly she put up her arms, but her heart was turning over in excitement.

"In that white dress?" His silvery glance skimmed her body, yet it was enough to make her blood sizzle.

"I'm not suggesting we get *too* close." She tried to make it sound light.

"Provocative little thing, aren't you?"

"I'm not that little." She looked at his tall figure. "Come on, Byrne. Be brave. There's no one around."

"And I'm pleased about that." He reached for her with something like extreme grace, clasping her willowy waist. A touch so light, yet it might have been a flame. He hadn't intended to do *anything*, sharply conscious of her shining appearance, only her body seemed to *flow* to him. There was heat, pleasure, an undermining rush of desire that made him feel immensely wary.

This is wrong, he thought. *All wrong*. He wouldn't be drawn into her spun silver web. Neither would he complicate her young life.

Her hand was on his shoulder, and though he tried to ease away they were moving with an exquisite spontaneous rhythm, her sweet, tuneful voice a soft ribbon of sound. It delighted him, gratifying some deep need.

"Isn't it romantic..." She half sang, half hummed the theme song from Audrey Hepburn's famous movie *Sabrina*, only the lightness she planned didn't quite come off. There was a thread of real emotion in her voice, betraying the fact she, too, was shaken with a pleasure she had never known.

Dancing with Byrne Beresford was the realisation of a dream. A zone of enchantment. She was mindless of her expensive dress. She wanted him to draw her closer, but just when it seemed he was about to throw off his restraint, his arms fell away abruptly, leaving her feeling almost rebuffed.

"I got a real kick out of that, Antoinette," he drawled.

She didn't need radar to detect the sexual animosity. "I'm convinced we could have done better." She tried to speak lightly, but he was all taut, suppressed energy.

"There are a few factors to be considered, Antoinette."

"Such as?" she asked innocently, looking at the same time extraordinarily desirable.

"I'm very much aware of your age and the fact you're about to join the family," he told her.

"How does that affect our dancing together?" She was flushed and excited.

"You should see your face. It's glowing."

She put an involuntary hand to her cheek. It burned. "I thought you liked my face."

"It should be on a coin." His tone was sardonic. "There's no use whatever trying to captivate me, Antoinette, so don't go putting your heart and soul into it."

She was surprised by her quiet rejoinder. "I would think captivating you would prove a very difficult business." She knew it sounded a little tart.

"You could handle it." He shrugged.

All of a sudden, heat suffused every pore of her skin. "You wouldn't consider placing bets, would you?" She watched his handsome mouth quirk.

"I never gamble when I can't guarantee the results."

"Then you're not a bit of fun, are you?" She looked at him through her long, curling lashes. At that moment pure Zoe.

"Scared, too." He smiled. Her sexuality, radiant as it

was, had an innocent, tremulous quality he found very sweet.

"Of me?" She couldn't stop her voice rising.

"A beautiful woman makes cowards of us all," he drawled.

"Oh, go take your shower." Exasperated, she turned away.

"The hell of it is, I need it." He laughed, amusement in his sparkling eyes. "I have to be careful, so careful, around you."

By noon most of the guests had arrived. Some flew in, some made the overland trek. In such a vast country most people thought nothing of a drive involving hundreds of miles of travel. The whole idea was getting there, and Castle Hill was famous for its polo parties. All the guests would be returning for the wedding, expected to be a clear winner in wedding-of-the-year stakes. Both young people were very popular, with many friends. The Beresfords numbered among the rich and legendary, the homestead was out of this world and therefore the big event was looked forward to with great anticipation. It was a chance, too, for the women to dress up, and they put their hearts, not to speak of their money, into planning their wardrobes.

They all met for lunch in the informal dining room set up for a buffet—ham, chicken, turkey, a side of smoked salmon with a variety of salads and something hot in covered dishes. It all looked delicious, Toni thought, her eyes skimming across the refectory table to the series of open French doors. Family and guests were assembled there or spilling onto the colonnaded terrace, immersed in conversation, which seemed to break off abruptly as she entered the room.

The return of the infamous Zoe Streeton's daughter, she thought, finding it painful when the plain truth of the matter was she couldn't have looked more lovely or more herself.

Joel made that perfectly clear, beating everyone to get to her. "An angel, as I live and breathe! Toni, how marvellous to see you again." He looked at her with smiling pleasure, blue eyes bright. At twenty-four Joel was almost as tall as his brother, but where Byrne had a powerful fully developed physique, Joel was lanky but with the Beresford good shoulders.

"It's lovely to see you, Joel." On a wave of warmth, Toni presented her cheek and Joel made the most of it, his lips lingering on her creamy skin, savouring it.

"I think you can take it, Toni, you've come up to Joel's expectations." Byrne joined them, looking at his brother with wry amusement.

Joel couldn't take his eyes off her. "You're so much like your mother," he said, his eyes very bright.

"Antoinette has her own identity," Byrne told him smoothly. "We're not going to let you monopolize her, either." He took Toni's arm with assured grace. "Come and meet the others, Toni. Most you'll know or remember."

The Beresford cousins, the watchful expression in their eyes at variance with the bright smiles. Tall, dark, long-limbed, with a strong familial look.

"Nice to see you again, Toni," Sally, the nicer one, said. "I love your dress. Did you buy that in Paris?"

"Yes." Toni smiled.

"I thought as much." Tara raised delicate brows. "I suppose you went to all the fashion shows?"

Toni smiled again. "Not likely. I could never get in."

She didn't say she had met several of the world's top models and found them very friendly and levelheaded.

Next came the polo players with their wives and girlfriends. Fern Patterson, sister to James, the captain of the opposing team. Fern was small, fair, with a stylish tousle of blond curls and a capable, intelligent little face. Although Toni liked the look of her, her radar detected that Fern was somewhat wary. It wasn't until later Toni found out why. Fern had been Joel's girlfriend for almost a year. Something of a record.

Andrea Benton was a surprise. Not pretty at all, yet by dint of know-how and discipline she managed to look striking. Tall, thin and tanned, she wore her expensive clothes well. Her light green eyes were very clear and direct. She had excellent teeth and a very attractive smile. But it was her hair that drew the most attention. Cut in a short medieval bob, it was an impossible but eye-catching burgundy. Cate later told Toni that Andrea changed the colour of her hair at the drop of a hat.

"I've heard so much about you, Toni." Andrea shook Toni's hand firmly. Her voice was good, well-pitched, educated, with that faint note of arrogance common to the very rich.

"I'm delighted to meet you, Andrea," Toni responded, wondering if what Andrea heard had been good. Andrea wasn't Byrne's type, but she seemed coolheaded enough to qualify and a strong contender in the social context.

While they stood chatting, Sonia, who had been having a few words with the housekeeper, hurried into the room. "Why don't we start lunch?" she suggested, smiling at everyone.

"You're going to sit beside me." Joel reappeared like magic at Toni's side.

"We have our allotted places, Joel," Byrne informed him mildly. "Surely you're going to sit beside Fern?"

"Hell, Byrne, I haven't seen Toni in years. You're not going to pressure me, are you?" Joel complained.

"Absolutely. Fern is looking a little lost. Go to her."

It was a pleasant lunch. Sonia as hostess was most gracious. But Toni couldn't throw off the sensation of being under review. Tara in particular seemed to want to lay a guilt trip on her. Joel, however, was in high spirits, his happy talk and enthusiasm infectious, causing Toni to burst out laughing on several occasions. It was obvious he was putting on a show for her even if her effect on him wasn't endearing her to certain people at the table. If Joel was trying to be the life and soul of the party it was Byrne to whom everyone turned like sunflowers to the sun. All the men were wearing polo gear. Byrne's team featured a navy polo shirt with distinctive lightning-bolt flashes in red and white. The opposing team wore dark green shirts with a vertical yellow stripe to one side. Every one of them to a man was tall, vigorous, physically attractive, but none had Byrne's extraordinary aura. It seemed to Toni he looked incredibly glamorous, his luminous gray eyes startling against his bronze skin and ink black hair. Catching Andrea's unguarded expression, Toni realised she wasn't the only one to think so. Andrea's green eyes shone brightly, fiercely, with a kind of raw hunger. Then she realised she was being observed and the shutters came down.

So now I know, Toni thought. *Andrea is out to make a brilliant marriage. Who can blame her?*

Andrea smiled and transferred her attention to Toni. "Do you intend going back to France, Toni?" she asked, her voice friendly, but a keen alertness in her eyes.

"We're going to do everything in our power to keep

her here," Cate called. "Kerry loves having her here, and I've always wanted a sister."

"You have us." Tara looked at her cousin with more than a hint of offense.

"Of course I have, but you know what I mean." Confident, Cate flushed slightly.

"I haven't decided as yet, Andrea," Toni said. "My mother is expecting me back." As she spoke she glanced at Byrne, handsome, graceful, relaxed, leaning back in his chair.

"And Zoe usually gets what she wants," he pointed out gently.

An hour and a half later they were assembled at the playing field, one of two polo fields on the station. The men were all competing. The women sought the shade of the stand that had been erected at one end of the field. Dotted around the field were station employees, anyone who had the afternoon free with wives and small children. Everyone was an avid fan of the game, and although it was a private match, with top-class players they knew they were in for an afternoon of excitement and drama. Sonia wasn't present, saying she had much to do, so the young women were left to become better acquainted.

"Sit beside me, Toni," Cate invited. She was a little unhappy with Tara's attitude, which was a mite too abrasive. Toni Streeton was hardly a stranger. She was Kerry's sister, chief bridesmaid and a guest in the house. All the bridesmaids had to get on. Nothing, absolutely nothing was going to spoil her wedding, Cate decided, though she wasn't surprised at the stance her cousins, both acutely aware of their social position, had taken. They had opposed Toni's being bridesmaid, after all.

"She didn't even come home for her father's funeral. Really!" Cate could still hear Tara's voice in her ears. "What on earth are we supposed to think of her? As for that dreadful, dreadful mother and her tatty life—"

"She's Kerry's mother, too, Tara, might I remind you?" Cate had answered directly, as was her way.

"But he's nothing like her. He's a Streeton through and through."

If Byrne hadn't backed her, which in the end settled it, Toni would not have made the wedding party, Cate thought, drawing her large straw hat down against the shimmering light.

Byrne's team won the first half at a canter, four to one. Joel, playing to the gallery, almost came a cropper a couple of times until his brother and captain called something that brought him back in control. Before the second half Andrea excused herself then rushed to where Byrne was changing his shirt. It was almost too embarrassing to watch. This marvellous man with his wonderfully fit and taut torso, the bronze skin lightly matted with dark hair, his smile a white flare as Andrea said something to him that made him laugh. Toni took a quick, deep breath, and Cate tipped her a wink.

"Gorgeous, isn't he? My own brother."

"Andrea feels the same."

"She's mad about him," Cate confided. "Out of *nothing,* really. Byrne's so darned self-contained. She was mad about him from the day she met him. You know how Byrne is. I can't count the number of women who've been in love with him, but Byrne makes promises to no one."

"Maybe he's too busy running a cattle empire," Toni said a little dryly.

"Well, we can't forget that, and the chain isn't all of

it, as you know, but we all want Byrne to marry. He once told me the best way to seduce a woman is to be rich. Do you think that's true?''

Toni considered. ''Perhaps a bit cynical. Certainly plenty of women look to financial security. A position in life. All I know is I could never marry without love.''

''It's a great start.'' Cate laughed. ''Kerry and I began all those years ago as best friends. We're best friends to this day. It took a little time for us to wake up to the fact that we wanted to be man and wife.''

''And I'm so happy for you, Cate.'' Toni's violet eyes shone with sincerity. ''I know your marriage is going to last forever. Divorce is so terrible.''

Something told Cate Toni had had a bad time of it those years with her mother.

The second half got under way, and Andrea returned, a glitter of excitement lending colour to her face. ''Byrne says they're making it too easy.''

''Maybe they'll come storming back,'' Toni said, not really believing it.

Byrne's team was on a roll. Finally, the captain of the opposing team, James Patterson, previously intimidated by his brilliant opposite number, hit a long drive that went straight between the goal posts.

On the field Byrne saluted him, grateful for stronger competition. Things picked up after that. Joel, still showing off, chased everything, thundering in and shouldering his opposite number's pony off the ball. Inevitably, as the spectators feared, his stick tangled with another player's and wound up between his pony's front legs before he cartwheeled out of the saddle.

Fern jumped to her feet, her hands over her mouth smothering her cry, but Joel was back in the saddle in a flash. The final chukker was the best of the match, although Toni had the impression Byrne was letting the other team get away with a few points. He didn't, however, intend that they should win. At the crucial moment he slammed a magnificent long drive that soared through the air and through the opposing team's goal dead centre.

The perfect strike.

The bell rang.

It was over.

"Isn't Byrne a superb player?" Andrea clapped her hands vigorously. "Congratulations. Well done." A cry from the heart that wasn't lost on anyone.

In the afternoon, while most of the others sought the swimming pool, Toni decided to go riding. She was wearing a brief two-piece swimsuit beneath her shirt and jeans in case she felt like taking a quick dip in one of the lagoons. She would have to wash her hair again, but she didn't care. It was wonderful in the saddle, breathing in the uncontaminated air, no pollution of any kind. She had only been home a few days after a break of nearly five years, yet it felt like she had never been away. Much as she had loved France and the other European cities she had visited, she had always felt an expatriate, someone away from home, that one place that haunted her heart. The desert wind sang to her. She loved the vast wilderness, the spinifex and mulga plains, the towering pyramids of red sand, the fantastic interlocking river system of billabongs, lagoons and creeks that made the huge riverine desert a prize beef-fattening region, a grazier's dream after rain. Before she had gone away the state had been racked by drought, but good rains had been recorded in the past year with the promise of more rain for the tropical north's wet season. It was these northern floodwaters that fed the channel country. Not one drop of rain had to fall locally for thousands of square miles to be irrigated. The rivers spread for miles, running fifty miles across in time of flood, yet only on rare occasions did the floodwaters reach the southernmost reaches, emptying into Lake Eyre, the lowest and driest part of the continent and paradoxically one of the largest inland drainage basins in the world, covering over a million square kilometers. Only twice in the century had Lake Eyre filled with water, first in 1950, then again in 1974, the greatest inundation in five hundred years. The aboriginal tribes of the territory feared the lake they called Katitanda and the dreadful snake that lived beneath the rippling white salt. They never went near it, with its incongruous arctic appearance of pack ice and endless snowfields, the extraordinary crystal formations that resembled ice flowerets and seashells. Byrne's father had flown scores of friends, including Toni's father, over the vast inland sea of 1974 so they could witness the great inundation. At such times there was lots of talk of harnessing the monsoonal rains of northern Queensland and diverting the waters by pipeline to the arid centre, but the monumental project had never been undertaken. She and Kerry had once camped at Lake Eyre with their father, setting up their tent on the white shores of the fabled inland sea. Once palms and cycads had grown there. The water had been fresh and blue. But that was long, long ago.

By the time she reached White Lady Lagoon, encrusted with splendid white water lilies, she was feeling the heat and ready for a swim. She left the gelding to enjoy the shade of a fine stand of coolabah trees, which grew only around the watercourses. She walked across the morning glory that draped itself all over the slopes in a haze of blue violet. She stepped out of her clothes, folded them neatly, then loosely braiding her hair she walked across the sandy white soil to the water. It looked so inviting, a vivid emerald green jewel-like in its clarity. She waded in to test the depth, her skin pleasantly tingling from the coldness of the water. The lagoon, which ran over a mile in length, had always been called the White Lady, just as other lagoons on this and other stations, including Nowra, were named for the colours of the beautiful water lilies that covered every billabong, creek and pond. Red, blue, creamy yellow and pink. Nature had bestowed a fantastic variety of wildflowers and water lilies all over the desert plains and watercourses. All it took for these ancient arid lands to bloom was water, and not particularly much of it. A passing shower would scatter the area with floral gems.

Toni, a strong swimmer from childhood, swam to the middle of the lagoon and looked toward the banks. The emu apples were bearing, their fernlike branches hung with the small round fruit the emus loved so much. Such a beautiful spot, she thought. Filled with strong magic. Her hair had slipped out of its braid, so she raised her hands to press its silky wetness from her face. When she lifted her eyes again, a shadowy figure was making its way through the trees, heading down the slope into the full radiance of sunlight.

Joel. Much as she liked him, she would have preferred to be on her own.

"Hi!" he called breezily, raising a hand in greeting. "I thought I'd find you here." The next minute he stripped down to a pair of swimming briefs, tossed his clothes aside and without another word hurled himself into the water, striking out for her with a powerful crawl. A moment later he was beside her, lifting his water-slicked head. "I couldn't resist coming after you. Marvellous, isn't it? You really know you're alive." He began to swim again, circling her slowly like a friendly dolphin. "I don't think I've had you to myself for fully five minutes since you arrived."

Something had to be settled right there. "Listen, Joel." Toni trod water, looking around vaguely. She expected any moment to see Byrne stalking toward them eyes like ice. "Isn't Fern your girlfriend?"

Joel's good-looking face suddenly wore a frown. "Sure, but I've got lots of girlfriends."

"Let's concentrate on Fern," Toni said. "I don't want you to forget about her."

He swam close. "Difficult with you here. You've returned like a swan. Come to think of it, that's the motif for the wedding. Two swans. They only mate once, as you know. Mamma's using that little mating ritual, the way they bend their necks to form a heart, for a lot of the decorations."

"How lovely!" Toni was diverted. She half shut her eyes, her face dreamy . "I can picture it clearly. Two beautiful white swans. A pity she couldn't have used our Australian black swans. They have white underfeathers, and red beaks but I suppose white is more appropriate for a wedding."

Joel groaned and shook the water from his hair. "The wedding! In a way I'll be glad when it's over. It's all that gets talked about. Even Fern has started to talk engagement. She's never done that before. All this wedding business has set her off."

"So I read the situation correctly." Toni looked up as a flight of corellas came to cloak the coolabahs in white. "You understand why I don't want to cause trouble? There were those who were against my coming back. You spoke of disagreements before. Who exactly voted for me to be bridesmaid?''

Put on the spot, Joel looked embarrassed. ''Cate wanted you, of course.''

''Not your mother?''

''Take it easy, Toni. That's not fair. Of course, Mamma. The big problem was...'' He hesitated.

''Zoe?''

''Byrne wanted you,'' Joel said, realising she was upset. ''I did, too, of course, but Byrne has the casting vote on everything.''

''I would have thought it was up to Cate and Kerry to make all the decisions.'' Toni's lotus eyes flared.

''Don't be angry, Toni. You wanted to hear.'' Then suddenly, because he didn't welcome problems, he said, ''Race you to the shore.''

''Fine. I can beat you anytime.''

Of course she didn't. It was impossible to beat such a strong male swimmer, but she made a creditable effort.

Joel rose from the water, turned and lifted her into the air. ''Don't I get a kiss for winning?''

''What do you think?'' Toni looked into those seemingly innocent blue eyes. ''Joel, put me down.''

''You're a featherweight! Is that a yes?''

''All right, on the cheek, as I'm to be a member of the family.''

''And it's wonderful,'' he said. He tilted her chin, surrendering eagerly, impulsively, to the pressing urge to drop a kiss on her lovely mouth, only at the last minute she turned her head.

''I mean what I say, Joel.'' Gently she pulled free.

''That's interesting. So do I.'' He couldn't stop himself from looking at her now that she was clear of the water. Her body was beautiful, nymphlike, delicate and feminine. Her breasts were small but delicious, her waist tiny, her hips narrow, her legs long, lovely and straight. He couldn't say why, exactly, but a vision of Fern in a swimsuit swam into his mind. Fern's compact body was almost boyish in comparison. Toni made him think of making the most wonderful love.

"Are you going to stop staring?"

His grin flashed. "I thought I was being subtle."

"No way! Don't you think we should get back?"

"What's the hurry?"

"I don't want any trouble, Joel. I suggest you finish with one girlfriend before you start with the next."

"You're worried about Fern, aren't you?" he called as she waded onto the sand.

"I told you. I don't enjoy hurting people. I'm worried about Byrne, as well. I'm only here for a month. I don't want to make waves."

"That must present a problem," a deep voice called sardonically from a little distance to their left.

They both turned abruptly, staring toward the shroud of trees. A heartbeat's pause, then Joel responded. "I might have known it would be you, Byrne."

"Oh, well," Byrne drawled, coming into view. "I don't particularly like having to hare after you, but Fern is distressed!"

Toni's colour rose at the implication. "I've got nothing to do with that." She walked quickly to her things. "Absolutely nothing."

"I realise that, Antoinette." Byrne took a moment to reach them, tolerance in his gray eyes. "We're dealing with Joel here. It's a little bit rough, isn't it, Joel, leaving Fern on her own?"

"Maybe, but she's not my wife," Joel protested, put out because he'd been having a wonderful time.

"I agree, but she feels quite rightly you owe her a little more courtesy."

"Oh, hell, can't she enjoy herself with the girls?"

"She didn't have much choice. You took off so abruptly. I'll admit it saved me a lot of time figuring out where you were heading. It might be an idea, though, if you headed back."

Joel looked shamefaced. "Okay, okay. I get the message. So what in the hell am I supposed to do, marry her?"

Byrne's smile was ironic. "No one is suggesting that, but don't run out on her, either. She's done nicely for a year."

"I don't like to be put on a leash," Joel muttered.

"The advantage of being male," Toni said, towelling herself off furiously. "I've never met one of you who didn't want to do what they damned well liked."

"You're not suggesting women don't." Byrne's tone was mild, but his eyes were like an electric charge.

"I'd better go." Joel, too, began flinging on clothes. "I left the Jeep a way back."

"Why?" Byrne turned to survey his brother. "Could it be you were trying to creep up on Toni?"

"I wanted to surprise her." Joel scooped up his shoes hastily.

"I'm sure you made a good job of it."

"See you later, Toni," Joel called, his expression regretful. "You could come back with me in the Jeep, if you like. Your horse can find his own way home."

"Goodbye, Joel," Byrne said firmly.

That settled it. Joel loved and respected his brother deeply. He spent most of his time trying to please him.

"I'm looking forward to dancing with you at the party, Toni," he called as he made his way up the bank.

Toni reached for her pink shirt, just missing it in her haste. Byrne picked it up and passed it to her, his mouth curled into a laconic smile. From the very first time at the hotel, his silver gaze had made her incredibly aware of her body. It was exciting and frightening at one and the same time. Her two-piece swimsuit, like her shirt, was pink, but a deep fuchsia, chic but not much in the way of coverage. She knew how she must look to him, from her long wet hair to her bare feet. The fact she had her jeans on would accentuate the skimpiness of her bikini top. Though it was hot, she felt her nipples peaking against the Lycra as though they were being stroked. If he hated women so much, why did he look at her like that?

Almost angrily she shouldered into the cotton shirt, doing up a button here and there but allowing it to hang out.

"Are you out to seduce me?" he asked.

For a moment she said nothing, nothing at all. "I'm sorry, Byrne. Too risky."

"But you admit the danger?"

"Sure I do, but I choose to resist it."

He stared at her. "You were having a glorious time with Joel."

"You were watching?" Her eyes kindled with blue fire.

"*Looking* for you would be closer to the truth. I saw the Jeep. I knew I'd find the two of you."

"Doing what?" She flushed. "Joel is nothing to me."

"And it has to stay that way, Toni." He reached out and stroked her hot cheek very gently, feeling the warmth bloom. A simple gesture, but it brought every fiber of her alive.

"*Why* exactly?" Despite herself, her voice was tremulous.

"A romance just isn't on. Joel has a lot of growing up to do. He's being incredibly insensitive where Fern is concerned."

"I'm aware of that, as it happens. What disturbs me is you think he's perfectly safe with Fern but I'm a moral danger." Temper was bubbling within her. Temper and a whole lot of feelings that were putting her under pressure.

"In a very short time, too." Byrne's tone was dry. "It's not your fault, Toni, but nothing is going to alter the fact your effect on Joel has been explosive."

"So what on earth am I supposed to do about it?" She looked at him. Looked away, startled at the expression she saw in his eyes.

"Tell him there's someone in Paris you miss terribly," he suggested.

"I see. *Lie.*"

"Didn't you tell me that there was someone called Akbar?" Slowly, disturbingly, he smiled.

"Don't be ridiculous. Akbar's only a friend."

"Lord, and I thought you made him up."

"I might as well go back now." Toni's tone was crisp. "There's no peace here."

"Really? I think it's beautiful. So restful."

"Do you bring Andrea here?"

His amusement faded. "Don't listen to gossip, Toni."

"Then it's not true?" She turned, wanting to goad him as much as he had goaded her.

"What?" He wasn't about to help her out.

"I spend a lot of time studying faces. I couldn't miss Andrea's adoration."

"That sounds painful. I'm not involved with Andrea yet. I've partnered her a few times at various functions."

"And made love to her once or twice?" The very thought left her dazed.

"You think that has something to do with *you?*"

"You're the guy who's interfering in *my* affairs." She stood her ground.

"Watch yourself, Toni," he said in a soft, dangerous voice.

"I don't toe the line for you, Byrne Beresford," she retorted with tart honesty.

"You will while you're here."

"Is that a threat?"

His eyes gleamed pure silver. "Of course it is." He pushed his Akubra back on his head, releasing a crisp lock of black hair onto his forehead. "Enjoy yourself all you want. Just don't steal Joel's heart away."

She made a strangled little sound in her throat. "Who said I was even trying? At least he's a risk taker."

"And you've identified I'm not?" He let his eyes rake her, while his heart most unaccustomedly gave a series of jolts.

"Sounds like it," she said sweetly.

"I've got more on my mind than falling for women, Antoinette." So why did he let his eyes settle on her mouth as if he was thinking of kissing her?

"Not *anyone?*" she asked carefully.

"*You're* my type, but it simply isn't possible."

That stunned her to silence. She put up a confused hand and drew back a straight, shining sheet of hair.

"Cat got your tongue?" he asked sarcastically, studying her intently.

She returned that beautiful sparkling gaze. "Actually for once I agree with you. But don't wait too long. Time whizzes by. You might wake up one morning and say, what the hell happened? Where's my wife and kids?''

He laughed. Pure male. Pure dynamite. God's gift to women. "I'll let you know when I'm ready to settle down. Who knows? I might even consider *you* when you grow up. But for now my life is packed.''

She felt so startled, excited, all sorts of things, she didn't quite know what she would say or do. Byrne Beresford to consider *her?* She nearly fainted at the idea, but worked hard to answer. "Are you saying you might consider me in time?''

"That depends entirely on you, Antoinette. I'd like you to know your own mind. Be a little wiser. Get it all together and so forth.''

She realised suddenly those brilliant, intimate eyes were dancing with amusement. "Are you sure you're not stalling for time?''

He was silent, looking over the shining waters of the lagoon. "You'll never believe this, but I'm afraid to think.''

She was familiar with that feeling. Everything was moving so fast. "And I'm talking wildly.''

"Don't apologise," he drawled. "I'm enjoying it.''

"You're not serious, either.'' Her chin went up. "You might consider you have absolutely no right to lead me on.''

"Oh, dear, don't I even get a smile?'' He moved to her, tipped her face for his inspection. "Don't be mad at me, Antoinette.''

Surely he knew his slightest touch made her quiver. She looked deeply into his eyes, trying to disentangle all his mixed messages, his motives. "I should be but I'm not.''

"And don't make a fool out of Joel," he added briskly, giving the point of her chin a little pinch.

That did it. She pulled away in utter exasperation. "Oh, goodness. I should have known. A tip for Toni."

He bent his rangy body to pick up her things. "Hey, I'm not trying to spoil your fun. Just a word of advice. You'd have my heart, as well, if you could figure out a way to do it."

"Well, it would be one way of getting square," Toni responded tartly.

"For what?"

She looked at him, unbearably handsome, sexy, the arrogant male. Hard to tell him, for all the magic he worked. Instead she said, "I'm off." She started up the grassy slope as if the devil himself was after her.

"Are you going somewhere or am I allowed to keep you company?" He caught her easily, laughter in his dark-timbred voice.

"This is your kingdom, Byrne Beresford. You're totally in control."

He caught her hand. Wouldn't release it, though she was desperate to pull away. "Not with you around, Antoinette," he said.

CHAPTER FOUR

TONI couldn't remember agonising more over her image for a party. She'd brought only one evening dress. Though it suited her beautifully, she was anxious it might be a little too dressy. For all her good looks she wasn't really one to flaunt them. She had a nonthreatening nature. She wanted the other young women to like her, not see her as competition. She felt sympathy for Fern, but there wasn't much she could do about that situation. Joel was still in his early twenties. He obviously needed time. Byrne was overreacting.

Because she had little option, she slipped the short evening dress over her head. It was a soft golden yellow in colour. A silk jersey sprinkled all over with tiny gold sequins, with the neck, hem and cutaway armholes defined by a gold border. Zoe's dressmaker, who had once worked for Chanel, had run it up for her.

"What's the point of being beautiful if you can't wear a gorgeous dress?" Francine had said.

It looked wildly expensive but Francine had only charged for the material as a gesture of friendship. Toni on many occasions had done favours for Francine. It seemed right to pull back her hair, cooler, too. In the last Paris collections the models had their long hair fashioned into updated knots, chignons, buns. The chignon worked best, arranged fairly low on her neck. The only jewelry she needed was a pair of earrings. The pearl and gold Zoe had given her.

As guest of honour, Toni found herself once again at

Byrne's side. Cate sat opposite her, Kerry alongside, with Andrea between him and James Patterson. For the gala occasion they were using the formal dining room, a very large room balanced by a magnificent Georgian mantel of white marble complete with a beautiful mirror, two splendid light-filled paintings of Venice, of all places, to either side. Toni, who had become something of a connoisseur, could identify the gleaming mahogany pedestal table and the elegant chairs as Regency, and there was a vividly toned antique Heriz carpet over the glowing parquet floor. Two beautiful arrangements of flowers stood at either end of the mantel, set with famille rose porcelain, and two exceptionally fine gilt and crystal chandeliers were suspended from the lovely molded ceiling. The table was set with Royal Crown Derby, the cutlery sterling silver, the wineglasses Baccarat, with pairs of silver candlesticks at intervals the length of a table, and with low floral arrangements, white lilies interspersed with butterfly orchids, Geraldton wax buds, ivy and magnolia leaves, all Sonia's doing. Sonia, in an ankle-length slim dress of silver moiré, held court at the opposite end of the table, with Fern and Joel nearby. *As far away from me as possible*, Toni thought.

It was a privileged world and it had strict rules. People like Zoe, who lowered the standards, would get swept under the carpet. Even Kerry, so much in love, looked a little uncomfortable in his evening clothes, but *handsome*, and nothing could dim his smile, Toni thought lovingly. It flashed, illuminating his young, tanned face, sparkling golden lights in his brown eyes. How like their father he was.

The conversation, as was to be expected at such a gathering, was lighthearted, a bit gossipy, nothing of great consequence, allowing them to enjoy the delicious meal served by Bridie's smartly uniformed and well-trained staff. Baby lobsters in a lime sauce comprised the entree, followed by seared marinated melt-in-the-mouth beef fillets served with a selection of fresh vegetables and a choice of desserts—ricotta, orange and mango tartlets served with thick cream or caramelized coconut cream with mango. Toni let the talk eddy around her, content to give herself up to the pleasure of fine wine in her mouth and beautifully presented, delectable food on her plate.

After dinner the young women retired briefly to the powder room to make a few running repairs, leaving the men to enjoy a few minutes of private conversation—business, the state of the economy, what federal minister should be sent packing and so forth, all washed down by an excellent port.

Toni waited her turn at the mirror to reapply a coat of lipstick as Andrea came alongside. Only the two of them were left, which Toni sensed was deliberate.

Andrea stood studying their reflections before she spoke. "You must have paid a great deal for that dress." For the first time her green eyes showed a trace of envy.

Toni saw it but responded pleasantly. "Actually a friend of my mother's ran it up for me."

"It's beautiful. Your mother... That would be the legendary Zoe." Andrea took out a compact and touched pressed powder to her nose and chin. "I've heard so much about her."

"From whom?" Ever defensive, Toni reacted a little shortly.

"Why, Byrne, of course," Andrea answered, as though surprised by such a question. "Forgive me, but you do realise Joel and Fern have been going together for the past year?"

"So?" Toni was puzzled.

"You're rather putting a damper on it." Andrea's voice was laced with censure.

Toni felt her patience slipping. "Maybe you're all putting too much pressure on him," she retorted.

"I gather you don't like being spoken to." Andrea flushed.

"You gather correctly."

Their conversation, scarcely amiable, was interrupted by a smiling Cate, who popped her head around the powder room door.

"Plenty of time for you two to become better acquainted." She smiled, totally unaware of any tension between her two bridesmaids. "It's time for dancing now."

She sounded so bright and excited Toni planted a smile squarely on her face.

The ballroom looked splendid, a forerunner for the great day. Four chandeliers blazed, the woodwork glowed and the huge room was fragrant with flowers. Kerry and Cate, looking wonderfully happy, were already whirling on the polished floor. Fern and Joel had joined them with another beautifully dressed couple. Joel put up a hand, waving, and Andrea turned to Toni with a tight smile. "Just remember what I said, Toni. Joel was happy before you came."

Andrea's assumption she was almost family quite took Toni's breath away.

"Andrea, I have nothing to answer for, and even if I did I wouldn't be answering to you," Toni said as calmly as she could. Across the room from them Byrne was talking to James Patterson. She had never seen anyone who exuded such crackling vitality. A quality that was palpable. He turned and saw them. She could hear his voice as he excused himself from James's side. He was coming toward them, Andrea quivering with expectation beside her. Which one would he ask to dance? Suddenly it seemed imperative to simplify things. Somebody else called her name. Heavens, it was Joel. He reached her before Byrne, holding out his arms.

"My dance, I think."

It was impossible to refuse him. Rude, as well. Joel was neither married nor engaged. Like his brother, it was apparent he was taking his time.

"You look gorgeous," Joel told her when they were out on the floor. "What was wrong with Andrea?"

"What do you mean?" Toni feigned surprise.

"It looked like you two were having words."

"Bad as that?" Toni wondered who else had noticed.

"Andrea doesn't cotton well to rivals."

"Are you saying she thinks I might want to take Byrne off her as well as you off Fern?" Toni asked with a breeziness she didn't feel.

".I don't think that would be asking too much." Joel grinned, abandoning himself to the pleasure of holding her.

Although Joel was clearly out to have fun, it was with a sense of relief Toni was claimed by one of Joel's friends. In fact, to no one's surprise, she was kept in constant circulation until she began to feel breathless.

Even then Joel, seeing her momentarily alone, moved across the vast shining floor to her, a moth to the flame, only to be forestalled as a man's arm reached for her. Beneath the dark cloth of his sleeve, bronze skin, hard bone, rippling muscle.

Byrne.

"You're not having a lot of success keeping Joel at arm's length." His eyes met hers, amused, half irritated.

"Don't blame me for Joel's exuberance," she said. "I wish he had your knack for keeping your distance."

"Does this mean you've missed me?" His voice was extraordinarily deep, dark, too damned sexy. It plucked her nerves like strings.

"I was expecting one dance, at least." She drew back slightly to look at him.

"Well, I don't think whirling off with Joel was the way to do it."

"Actually, I didn't know who you intended to dance with. Me or Andrea. I decided to make your choice simple."

"Am I supposed to feel grateful?" He held her still for a moment, looking at the long, slender line from her throat to her breasts.

"Yes. Very. I'm sure you're aware I've started up a whole lot of tension?" Even as she spoke she caught sight of Fern and Joel by the door, Fern's expression one of suppressed indignation.

"Well, you're much prettier than all of them," he said lazily, thinking Joel would never respond to a tight leash. "Why don't we go out onto the terrace for a breath of air? I'll fetch us a glass of champagne."

"That would be lovely." She suddenly relaxed and smiled at him.

Within a moment he rejoined her and both of them moved onto the colonnaded terrace where the air was beautifully cool and balmy and the Milky Way streamed down the sky in a river of diamonds. Toni wandered toward the garden to inhale the scent of the massed gardenias. Being with Byrne was like basking in the sun after a frigid European winter. She sipped her champagne, wondering if he had the slightest inkling she was irretrievably in love with him. Had been for a huge part of her life.

"Such a beautiful night!" She lifted her face to the luminous sky. High above her, almost directly over the house, hung Kirrunjoonga, the Guiding One, the Southern Cross in all its glittering splendour, Orion, the mighty hunter endlessly in pursuit of the Seven Sisters. In a part of the world where the stars were exceptionally brilliant, she felt transported by their beauty. At the same time her nerves were aquiver. Proximity to this man filled her with happiness, excitement and a whole lot of emotional confusion. Maybe it was a legacy from Zoe, this sensual awareness.

"You stand out like a star yourself." He raised his glass to her, savouring her beauty, the swan's neck, its purity revealed by the unfamiliar hairstyle.

"Thank you, Byrne," she said simply.

"Great hair, great face. Great body. Long legs. A mind of your own."

"You don't think there's a danger in that?" she asked.

He looked at her. "Not in the least. I like women with their own voice."

"Maybe I should get involved in politics," she suggested.

"My mother is a strong force in the country women's movements," he answered as though suddenly considering it.

"Then you would expect that in your wife?"

Another pause. "Yes, I would."

"What else would you like?" She turned to him, the light a nimbus around her silver gilt hair and creamy face.

"Let's see." He stood looking at her. "A woman who could run on her own efficiency. A woman I could ab-

solutely trust. A woman I'd be lost without. A woman
with the sweetest smile. The softest mouth. Tender, loving, concerned. A woman who wants children. Our children.''

''You want a lot.'' There was the faintest tremble in
her voice.

He shrugged his wide shoulders. ''Marriage has to be
the biggest decision in life.''

''Lord, you should tell that to my mother.'' She
sighed heavily.

''You're someone else entirely, Antoinette.''

It was a comment she took to her heart. Hands on the
timber railings, she looked at the stars. ''In the
Dreaming, long ago, Meeka the Moon was married to
Ngangaru the Sun. They lived in a cave with their children. In time they became the stars.''

''The starry floor of heaven,'' he quoted. ''There's not
a star in the sky that doesn't have an aboriginal myth to
account for its origins. The constellation Scorpio up
there was originally two lovers who broke tribal law.''

''Oh, Byrne, look, a falling star!'' She put out her
hand, caught his sleeve, heart leaping.

''All the brighter in the falling. You'd better make a
wish.''

Let him love me. She never gave it a conscious
thought. It came spontaneously from deep within her.

''Tell me,'' he urged, watching her dreamy expression.

''I can't. It mightn't come true.'' She turned to smile
at him, sweet enchantment. He almost pulled her into
his arms, feeling the responsive stirring of his body. He
wanted to close his hands over those delicately boned
shoulders, bring his mouth down hard over hers, explore
its soft siren shape. He wanted to caress her small, high

breasts. Lift her. Carry her away. He felt his control begin a headlong slide. How had she done it? In its way it was like ceding command, and he wasn't a person who could easily accommodate such an upheaval in his life. Love, yes. But this fierce, demanding necessity of heart and flesh? It smacked of obsession.

Deliberately he faced the garden, looking out over the kingdom that was Castle Hill. "Have you thought any more about what you intend to do?" He knew his tone was crisp, almost businesslike. A far cry from the intensity of a few minutes before.

She was instantly aware of his withdrawal. She was engaged in trying to stem the violent inrushes of sensation. "Not really. I've touched only briefly on my affairs with Kerry."

"You mean about selling your share of Nowra?"

She took a cooling sip of champagne, set it down. "You're moving too quickly, Byrne, even for you."

"I'm only trying to help."

"Cate and Kerry. Not me."

"Why would you say that?" He barely trusted himself to look into her beautiful eyes.

"Cate is your sister. It's only natural you'd want to see her mistress of her own home."

"Of course, but you have no intention of living there. You said so yourself."

For an instant he thought she wouldn't reply.

"I don't want to give up all that's left of my father," she said finally.

That hit him forcibly. Didn't he still crave his father's company, his advice, their long discussions, their shared vision? "I can understand that, Antoinette."

"Can you?" She turned to him. "Then why are you so hard?"

"God knows!" He shrugged. He shouldn't start this, but this girl, this woman was having such an effect on him, he didn't doubt for a moment she would change his life radically. "Having you here has stirred up a lot of emotion," he said. "Brought back a lot of memories."

"How my father died?" she asked, her eyes clouding.

It wasn't quite what he meant. "None of us is going to forget that, Toni. I was the one who flew him to Base Hospital. I was the one who acted too late."

His words stunned her. "How could you possibly blame yourself?"

He spoke somberly but with pent-up emotion. "I know it's not quite rational, but I do. He'd told me how he gashed himself, on the two-way radio. I warned him about keeping up his tetanus shots. I should have taken the helicopter over."

The tension in her throat made it hard for her to swallow. "I didn't know you were carrying all this trauma, Byrne."

"Antoinette, there's a lot you don't know." Once again harshness crept into his voice. What was it he was trying to do? He didn't understand it. She wasn't responsible for anything that had happened.

"I'm sorry." She turned away swiftly, hiding sudden tears.

"Don't." He caught her hand, feeling the blaze of treacherous desire, hot, sweet, fierce. He was losing his head over this girl. "I keep forgetting how young you are."

Her fine, small hand was trembling. "Young in years, maybe, but I've learned what life is all about."

"It's insane for us to fight," he said.

"I think we're going to do a lot of it."

"No, you're overreacting." His warm grip tightened.

"I don't think so." She felt a little desperate under the weight of emotion. "I can see how you might think I threaten this happy time for Cate."

"Toni." Flat denial was in his voice. "All I've asked you to do is not encourage Joel. You can see he's enormously susceptible."

"And obviously you can just *trust* me. You're awfully rough on me, Byrne."

"Toni, don't rush away."

She felt his hand on her arm, long-fingered, warm, strong. "Please let me go."

"I can't do that." God, it was true. For a moment, caught in a desperate hunger, he couldn't release her. He was moving her into his arms. No force, but most compellingly. For all her high talk she didn't seem to be resisting. It was happening so fast. It was emotion ignited like a flame in dry grass, revealing the secret shadowy places of the heart.

Only a woman was watching them from the French doors, her body silhouetted against the brilliant lights that spilled from the ballroom, her smooth cap of hair a flaming burgundy.

"Byrne, I was wondering where you'd got to." Andrea did a wonderful job of keeping her tone light.

Laughter and music came to them on a sudden wave of sound. Odd, he thought, when only a few minutes before they might have been enclosed in a capsule full of silence and intense emotion. "Taking a breath of fresh air, Andrea. Want to try it?" he asked dryly.

"It's wonderful out here." Andrea sounded bright when inside she was pierced by jealousy. *Like mother, like daughter,* she thought. This Toni Streeton was taking everything from her, the party, her friends, her man.

"If you'll both excuse me…" Toni tried to make her escape. Her heart pounded in her breast, her whole body made aware of its urgent hungers.

Andrea nodded her approval. "Yes, the others are feeling quite deserted."

"Others?" Toni paused, keenly aware of Andrea's jealousy.

"I suppose I shouldn't say this, but there's Joel. He seems to have forgotten he's already taken." It was said in the most playful way possible, but Toni felt the sting.

"We've never heard that from him, Andrea." Byrne intervened, sounding so nearly curt Andrea's smile faltered.

"But surely they're very serious?"

"Fern may be serious," he corrected. "Joel's not quite managing it."

Toni left them to it. She walked quickly inside, relieved beyond words when the first person she saw was her brother.

Happy himself, Kerry took seconds to absorb his sister's expression. "What's up?"

"Nothing." Toni wasn't about to spoil his evening.

Kerry gazed past her to the terrace. "Don't tell me Andrea said something to you? I saw her go out looking for Byrne. He was with you?"

"Yes," Toni answered as calmly as she could. "We went out in search of air."

"Lordy, Lordy, she's mad about him, you know."

"I realise that, Kerry," Toni said with faint acerbity. "One would have to be blind and deaf to miss it."

"So what did she say?" Kerry stared at her.

"I'd just as soon drop this," Toni said firmly. "I don't want to mar this happy occasion."

Kerry reached for her hand, squeezed it. "Don't

worry, we'll be going home tomorrow. It's the wedding that's thrown everybody. It's an emotional time. The magic is there, but a lot of tension, as well."

"I'm so glad you found Cate." Toni looked at her brother earnestly.

"She's the only girl I've ever wanted." Kerry smiled. "No one knows me better, outside my sister. I don't want you to go away, Toni. I don't want to lose you, ever."

Most of the guests left the following morning, except Andrea and the Beresford cousins, who took themselves off to the pool to relax. Toni, who had been thinking of riding, abandoned the idea when Sonia suggested she might like to try on her bridesmaid gown.

"Just to be sure it's not in need of some small alteration, dear."

"First you have to see *my* magical dress." Cate smiled radiantly. She put out her hand to touch her mother's cheek. "It made Mummy cry."

"Because you're so beautiful in it, my darling, my only daughter. Go with Cate, Toni. I have a few things to attend to here, then I'll be up. Use my room so you can have a good look at yourself, Toni. There's a wall of mirrors."

They were walking up the staircase when Kerry came in. "Ah, there you are, my favourite girls. Feel like taking a ride?"

"In maybe fifteen minutes," Cate replied. "I want to show Toni my wedding dress first."

"So let's make that an hour," Kerry drawled laconically.

"No, fifteen minutes will be fine. Hang on," Cate corrected herself. "Toni has to try her dress, as well."

"That's okay. You two go ahead," Toni said. "Which direction are you riding? I'll catch up."

"It's a perfect day." Kerry smiled. "Why not the Five Mile?"

"Fine."

Cate's bedroom, which had a fine view of Castle Hill, was decorated in apple green and white with an array of Victorian botanical watercolours adorning the walls. There was a sofa and two deep armchairs, a small circular table, a very pretty antique dressing table near the door and a tall bookcase painted white filled with dozens of books and here and there charming ornaments. A lovely large room for the daughter of the house. "The dresses are in here," Cate said, making for the adjoining dressing room. "When we've finished with them they'll go back to the attic. We've had them hanging up there swathed in muslin. Sit down, Toni and I'll show you my fantasy."

When she returned she was carrying an exquisite bridal gown in lustrous, luminous magnolia duchesse satin.

"Cate, how beautiful!" Toni stood up, her face wearing an expression of absolute delight.

"I knew you'd think so."

Toni touched a reverent hand to the full, billowing skirt. It sprang from the fitted bodice, satin roses forming the heart-shaped strapless neckline. The bust was decorated with exquisite champagne lace, hand-beaded with crystals and hung with drop pearls.

"There's a lovely headpiece to go with it," Cate said excitedly. "A coronet of satin roses with a short full veil."

"You'll take Kerry's breath away when he sees you."

"That's what I'm hoping for." Cate smiled. "You know we're having a swan theme?"

"Yes. Joel told me."

"Swans mate forever," Cate said dreamily. "That's what our marriage is going to be."

"That's my wish for you." Impulsively Toni leaned forward and kissed Cate's cheek.

"*You* deserve a good life, Toni," Cate said, her eyes sparkling with a few happy tears. "It hasn't been easy for you."

"I've had my moments, Cate."

Cate's voice was soft. "Don't go away, Toni. Don't go back."

"I can't move in with you guys." Toni laughed, touched by the fact Cate wanted her.

"Toni, it's half your house," Cate said simply. "The last thing I would ever do is chase you away. You're very important to us. Kerry missed you terribly."

Toni flushed and turned away. "Yet he sounded very remote whenever I called. Many of my letters he didn't answer. I really thought I'd lost him, Cate."

"Kerry suffers in silence," Cate replied. "He's got a lot locked away inside him."

"Not many of us haven't. I'm very grateful to you, Cate, for the way you've eased his pain."

"Now we're getting too serious," Cate tried a smile. "You want to try on your dress."

In her bedroom, Toni stood looking at the beautiful bridesmaid gown as it swayed on its hanger. Like Cate's dress, the fabric was rich delustered duchesse satin, the colour an exquisite, indescribable blue-violet. The dress was strapless, but for the ceremony there was a little guipure bolero that left the shoulders bare and fitted snugly to just below the bust. The bodice was beautifully boned. She wouldn't need a bra. With a sense of plea-sure, Toni removed the yellow cotton dress she had worn for breakfast, standing briefly in her panties before she stepped into the lovely gown. The skirt billowed out from a dropped waist that met at a point centre front. The colour, the cut, the rich, gleaming fabric were everything. She moved to the antique pier glass on its mahogany stand. She could see most of herself. Not the wide view, and the bedroom lighting was rather soft. She reached for the lace bolero, put it on, admiring the way the lace was cut to frame her bare shoulders. There were satin pumps, dyed to match the fabric to create a total look. It was a gorgeous dress, marvellously flattering. It would be nice to have a really good look at herself under stronger lights. Sonia had offered.

Outside Sonia's room she knocked on the door, waited, and when there was no answer turned the knob and glided in. One didn't simply *walk* in a gown like this. Sonia had a suite with a sitting room on one side and a dressing room and bathroom on the other. The dressing room was large, with plenty of room to stand back and survey herself in the floor-to-ceiling mirrored wall.

She turned on the bright interior lights, watching their brilliance bring her beautiful gown to full, glowing life. For a split second she didn't recognise herself. In that sea of colour, her long hair shimmered as though it was stranded with sequins, a mix of silver and gold. There was a flush of excitement over her cheekbones, and her eyes glittered, gemlike, their colour intensified by the rich sheen of the satin. What magic a beautiful, romantic gown could weave. She leaned forward to stare at herself, even breathed on the glass to make sure she was real. Turning slowly as if in some courtly dance, Toni gathered her hair this way and that, wondering how it would best suit her floral headdress—falling loose, on top of her head, a coil low on the nape. Beautiful as her bridesmaid dress undoubtedly was, how much *more* wonderful would it be to stand in her own wedding dress, dreaming of the moment when she would look into the face of the man she loved with all her heart. The man who was part of the very fabric of her life.

As the thought spun through her mind, an image flashed, was caught, suspended in time.

She saw a face, lost herself in a pair of silver gray eyes. His ebony head was bent over hers, his wonderful mouth, so clean cut yet so sensuous, seeking to find hers. Anticipation was so palpable she gave a little gasping breath, then in the next second laughed at herself for being such a fool. She had to acknowledge she was in a very vulnerable state of mind, and all in the space of a handful of days. What was it? A predestined decree of fate?

Humorously, Toni returned to studying her reflection. The waist of the tight-fitting bodice was tiny, a seeming hand span against the billowing fullness of the skirt. The little lace bolero looked lovely, but she took it off, laying it gently over the back of a gilt chair. Without it the dress became a strapless ball gown, beautifully cut, incredibly glamorous. She could wear it over and over, which was the whole idea. Perhaps have the bodice hand sewn with crystals. Francine was marvellous at beading.

It took her a moment to realise someone had come into the adjoining bedroom. Sonia, probably, come to see how she looked. Shaking her hair free, one hand gathering up her billowing skirt, Toni moved to the bedroom, her heart leaping when not Sonia's but Byrne's voice suddenly called.

"Where the devil are you, Mamma?" His tone was

affectionate, casual, with the faintest hint of impatience. "I've just remembered we haven't—"

He was brought up with a tremendous jolt as once again she stole his breath.

"Byrne!" She seemed to be trembling, swaying like a lotus lily on its stalk.

"I'm sorry. I was looking for Sonia." He forced himself to speak lightly, but it passed beyond that to a kind of curtness. Better safe than sorry, he consoled himself. For both of us.

"She said she had a few things to attend to." Toni drew a long breath, dizzied by the expression in his brilliant eyes. "I was just trying on my bridesmaid gown."

"So I see." For a long moment he allowed himself to look at her. He had seen the dress, of course, the day it arrived, and later hanging from a high beam in the attic. Cate and Sonia had shown him dozens of swatches of material in the early days, beautiful materials, seeking his approval, as though disapproval was possible—whatever his sister wanted for her wedding day she was to get. But his only lasting impression had been a blur of luminous colours and rich fabrics. Now before him was Antoinette Streeton, a young woman he had known from childhood, dazzling him with her beauty. There was such a bloom on her flawless skin, skin that had the fragrance of frangipani. Her colouring was exquisite, shades of gold and cream, the tint of rose, the quite marvellous violet-blue of her eyes. It pierced his senses, beat in his veins. Her bare shoulders and the upper slopes of her young breasts rose out of the strapless gown, a rose-tinged shadow at the dip of the heart-shaped neckline.

"You look glorious," he said in a dark, moody voice, picking up a long lock of her hair, handling it. "The most beautiful woman I've ever seen." His tone turned ironic, slightly harsh. "One of those young women of poetry and legend. Rapunzel, Beatrice, the Lady of Shalott."

No matter how he tantalized her, the things he said, it was madness to dream he really wanted her. But what was she to read in his eyes?

"I'm glad you like it." Her voice was strained. Her nerves wound themselves into a tight ball.

"I like *you*." His eyes touched her hair, her face, her mouth, her throat, her breasts.

"So sad, then, you're making such an effort not to."

"I'm used to protecting my bachelor freedom."

"I know." The intensity of his gaze was disturbing her, but she didn't look away. "But you have a dual nature. I've sensed that all along."

"I can't get involved with you, sweet Antoinette. Not even for a little while."

"But you're being tested all the same?"

A trace of derision touched his mouth. "You know it. I know it."

"All I want is for you to see I'm a woman." Arms uplifted, she whirled, inviting his attention.

"You're playing with fire, Toni," he warned. "Fire burns."

"I know," she said simply. "But I'm drawn to it all the same."

"That was said with an air of fatalism."

She twirled very close to him, dipped a curtsy. "You don't believe in fate?"

He did now. "Down deep I suppose I do," he drawled, "but we have a will of our own."

"To fill our lives, surely. To take on adventure, ambitions, new challenges?"

"Antoinette. You *cannot* challenge me."

She stopped abruptly, as though recognising that was true. "No, of course not. I know all about the misery that comes from misguided passions." She went to sweep past him, so emotional it shocked her, only at the last moment he reached for her and drew her strongly against him as though to still her trembling. His tall, lean body was charged with such energy it was like an outside force driving him.

A convulsive little cry tore from her throat, a mix of panic and violent excitement. What a tumultuous business it was battling attraction. She had scarcely time to look at him before his mouth overwhelmed hers, crushing it so she could hardly breathe.

She seemed fragile in his arms, clinging to him so she could stand. Her heart was racing—he could hear its beating in his ears. He had never experienced such consummate pleasure. This had been waiting for him, indeed, staring him in the face. His tongue moved beyond her small white teeth, exploring deeply the moist interior. He could still breathe in the scent of frangipani. It seemed to emanate from her body. Desire for her mounted so swiftly there didn't seem a thing he could do about it. It was like a great flare of red. Red for passion. Red for *danger.*

"Don't they say the best way to get rid of temptation is to give in to it?" He wrenched up his dark head, his eyes blazing at her. She seemed dazed, unmoving, unable to answer. He shook her slightly. "Toni?" Intensely, he stroked her cheek.

"What is it?" Her voice was soft and weak.

"I hadn't intended this. But I can stop it." There was a hard, edgy note to his voice.

Her heart palpitated with pain. "Why are you being so cruel?"

"Cruel?" He looked at her with a mixture of anger, regret, desire, all doing battle in his dark, handsome face. "I'm trying to retain some control. You're not *ready* for this."

"I just don't know how you could say that," she protested.

"Because it's what I believe."

"So you alternate between pushing me away and going off the deep end?" Tears stood in her violet eyes.

"That's what worries me," he said. "The deep end. It should worry you, too."

"May I go, Byrne? I need to go." It was a plea.

She looked so young, so heartbreakingly beautiful, her eyes suffused with a glittering blue light. He spoke with passionate intensity. "I'm not going to hurt you, Toni."

"You have already."

"I truly hope not." His voice was eloquent.

"Don't worry," she said. Pride made her fling up her head. "I'll soon be off your territory. I like it a lot better in Paris."

"You'll never make a convincing liar."

"I don't belong here." Her ash-blond hair flew around her flushed face. "I have nowhere I can lay my head."

The truth of it struck him forcibly. "I'll make it right for you, Toni. I promise." He had a powerful urge to shield her from all harm.

"Oh, no." She shook her gilded head. "I want nothing from you, Byrne." Even as she said it she was shaking with a desire so intense she thought she might faint.

"You want what I want," he said harshly. "Whether it's good for us is another matter."

"So why won't you let me go?" she cried.

For the first time he registered that his arm was locked

around her small waist. "Because I'm too damned screwed up," he rasped. "I have been from the moment I laid eyes on you."

"Good!" Now her voice was touched with a tinge of hysteria. "The mighty Byrne Beresford has finally learned about torment. And I'm the cause of it. Can you imagine? Little Toni Streeton, the kid who was in love with you when she was seven."

"What do you mean *was?*" He reacted fiercely, pulling her to him, his silver eyes so bright they could have lit up the world.

This time she didn't even manage a cry. His mouth came blisteringly over hers, kissing her until the excitement grew too much to be borne. The tips of her breasts flared against the tight satin bodice, and he brought up his hand.

"Byrne!" Her eyes were shut tight against the rapturous agony.

"I want you," he muttered. He could have lifted her with one arm. Carried her off.

It was a measure of their intense involvement that they came perilously close to being surprised by Sonia.

"Toni? Are you there, dear?" she called, her voice growing stronger as she moved from the hallway into her large bedroom.

Toni's whole body flamed. The electricity between herself and Byrne was so strong it was palpable, causing the very air to crackle. Sonia would notice. She *had* to.

"Ah, there you are!" Sonia sailed into the room, her expression showing first surprise that Byrne was there, then a certain alarm. "Everything all right?" She looked from one to the other, noticing that her imperturbable son had a pallor beneath his dark copper tan and Toni's eyes were like saucers in her pale, creamy face.

They were standing very close together, yet their bodies seemed to be saying they desperately wanted to be somewhere else. Sonia fancied there was a glitter of unshed tears in Toni's eyes.

It was Byrne who answered, his striking face wearing its high, mettled look, his voice suave. "Of course, Mamma. Why wouldn't it be? Toni's been trying on her bridesmaid dress, as you see."

Sonia forced herself to speak casually. Toni still looked at a loss. She seemed to be trembling. "And it looks wonderful on you, dear. Show me." With the greatest effort Toni whirled for Sonia's inspection when she really wanted to sink through the floor. Sonia, too, strove to control her feelings of alarm. The room exuded so much emotion. She felt her first stab of jealousy. She doted on Byrne, her firstborn. She loved all her children, but it was Byrne who filled her with wonderment, Byrne who had realised her husband's and her dreams, Byrne who made her most conscious of the glory of motherhood. Now young Toni Streeton. A girl Sonia realised she might have difficulty accepting into the family. Not because she was Zoe's daughter. That was too unfair. But because Toni was one of those young women who stole a man's heart away. Stole all their love. Ashamed of her human frailty, Sonia continued, "It's a perfect fit, too. I'm so pleased."

Byrne put out his hand slowly, tipped Toni's chin. "Talk, at least," he prompted her, "otherwise we'll begin to wonder if you're an angel come to visit."

I hate you, Toni thought. *Tormentor.* Every nerve in her body leaped to his touch.

"I'm no angel. Count on it." She met his eyes with determination.

"Well, you look like an angel, more than anything else."

"Byrne, stop teasing," Sonia admonished, stuck with the feeling she wasn't even in the room. Something had been going on. Something disturbing. Not that the girl didn't look miraculous, drawing all the light in the room to herself. Hair, skin, eyes. Useless to deny a beautiful young woman's power. On the other hand, Byrne would be impossible to resist.

"Anyway, there was something I wanted to speak to you about, Mamma." Byrne turned and gave her a smile.

"I'll go change," Toni said.

She made to escape, only Byrne's powerful figure blocked her path. "We'll be breaking in the best of the brumbies this afternoon," he said quickly and casually. "Want to come?"

He must be crazy, she thought. *I must be crazy.* "I don't have anything else to do."

"Fine." He stood aside, smiling at her a little mockingly. "We'll be at Ibis Creek. Make it after lunch. I'll have one of the boys saddle up Rinka for you."

Rinka? Sonia took care not to pass a remark. Rinka was a lovely horse, a bright chestnut filly with wonderful bloodlines. Did the girl realise the honour?

Apparently she did. Toni swept away, flushed and radiant.

CHAPTER FIVE

EVERYONE was in for a light buffet lunch except Byrne, who seemed to survive on an excellent early morning breakfast and cups of tea with his men.

"Where is he, anyway?" Andrea asked. "There's a man who loses himself easily."

"He's got a lot of territory to lose himself in." Kerry smiled and leaned back. "Ten thousand square kilometers. I guess you could call that a spread."

"A big spread," Andrea acknowledged, obviously miffed she was missing out on his company. "But he must be hungry,surely? Are you sure no one knows where he is? I'd really like to speak to him before I leave."

"Why, he's at the Five Mile," Sonia volunteered.

"That's Ibis Creek?" Andrea asked, folding her napkin briskly.

"Come on, Andrea. You don't like a lot of dust flying," Joel teased.

"That's all right, I've adjusted to it. What's happening?"

"They're breaking in the best of the brumbies," Toni said, not comfortable with holier-than-thou Andrea. "Singing to them, talking them in. More endearments than threats. Horses need to know they're among friends."

"Come on then," Joel said happily. "Let's go. Toni, you're coming for sure."

"Byrne has already asked her," Sonia said. "She's to ride Rinka. Quite an honour."

"Good," Cate said, with instant approval. "Toni always was a darn good rider, even as a kid."

"I don't imagine she's been doing much riding in Europe," Andrea said.

"On the contrary, I've had access to a large estate. Not vast like our part of the world, but plenty large enough. And surpassingly green and beautiful."

Toni was at the head of the central staircase before Andrea caught her. "Why did you have to leave it to Sonia to tell me where Byrne was?"

"Why? Because Sonia is our hostess and Byrne's mother."

"What a cop-out," Andrea exclaimed. "It makes no sense his allowing you to ride Rinka, either. He'd never let me."

"Maybe he thought you weren't right for the horse," Toni half-joked.

"No, please, jokes aside," Andrea said, sounding distressed. She laid a restraining hand on Toni's arm. "I don't normally do this, but I feel I must speak out. I'm not an unfair person. I didn't judge you before you arrived."

"Judge me? What do you mean?" Toni felt she'd had enough of this.

"Well, so many aspects of your life, your mother's life arouse painful emotions. Being so close to Byrne, to the family, I couldn't help but hear about them."

"I'm sure Byrne has never discussed my family with you."

Andrea's thin, elegant face tightened. "Really, you're tremendously touchy."

"Only when I'm under attack. I can see you're worried you might be losing Byrne, Andrea, but directing your anger and aggression at me won't help. Either he cares about you, or he doesn't. We both know there's a distinction between fantasy and reality. You're not the first or the last to fall madly in love with Byrne Beresford. It's been happening ever since I can remember."

Silence. "Why don't you just pack your bags and go home," Andrea said very quietly, unable to handle the idea all her efforts at attracting Byrne might have been in vain.

"I *am* home, Andrea," Toni said and knew, finally, it was true. "I'm going to build my life here."

"This weekend isn't working out as smoothly as was planned, is it?" Joel asked, looking across at Toni sitting so easily in the saddle. She looked wonderful on Rinka, both of them so bright and colourful.

"No," Toni replied, her eyes on the grand sight of a flight of budgerigar on the wing.

"Are you really going back, Toni?" Joel asked tentatively.

She nodded. "Maybe for a while. Just to satisfy myself Zoe is all right."

"She's a grown woman, for God's sake!" Joel said scornfully, shoving his hat over his eyes.

"She's a woman. She's every inch a woman, but a *particular* woman. She doesn't know how to look after herself."

"Well, it certainly made things hard for you," Joel said with sympathy. "What's with you and Byrne?"

"In what way?" Toni was instantly on the defense.

"There's something between you two," Joel said. "I'm not such a damn fool I can't spot it."

"Your imagination is working overtime," she said lightly.

"So you won't level?"

"Does it matter to you?" She turned her head.

Joel's attractive voice was firm. "Toni, I'm interested in you myself. I thought I made that perfectly plain."

"You certainly made it plain to Fern."

"Whatever my sins, I've made no promises to Fern. She's a nice girl. I like her a lot. We've been seeing quite a bit of each other, but I've always been hoping for that lightning bolt. What do the French call it? You should know."

"*Coup de foudre*," Toni said, giving it an authentic French polish.

"Don't ever lose that accent." Joel smiled.

"I suppose in the end I will."

He looked at her, slightly puzzled. "This must seem pretty tame to you after all Europe has to offer."

"Does it seem tame to you?"

"I'd never want to be anywhere else."

"The same for me. The Big Sky Country is in our blood."

By the time they arrived at the campsite on the banks of Ibis Creek, a place visited by the sacred white ibis and the great blue cranes, the brolgas, a small crowd had arrived, drawn by the interest and excitement of seeing the best of the draft learn to handle their loss of freedom. From a *master*. These were wild bush horses, used to calling the vast open plains their territory. Thousands of them roamed the station, some far out into the desert with only the dingoes, the kangaroos and the wild camels to keep them company, all of them descendants of the station horses that had escaped from the beginning of settlement until the present day, when the reigning stallions came in search of fresh station mares. A mob of about thirty was being held in one of the yards. Byrne was working a fine-looking bay colt, swinging an old burlap bag gently back and forth.

Immediately Joel went to join Cate and Kerry, who were sitting on the top rung of the fence with Andrea, swathed in a head scarf, a large straw hat and huge sunglasses, alongside. All three had driven out in the Jeep, arriving long before Toni and Joel. Twenty or more people were scattered around the area, including the four head stockmen, who ran the mustering camps, a couple of the jackeroos, one a young Englishman of distinguished family who had begged his father for a year of adventure before returning home to take up serious study, and the wife and young children of Perky Parkins, a part aboriginal stockman and a marvelous horse handler. Although he was only in his twenties, Perky was so good the rest of the aboriginal stockmen called him "old man," a term of respect. Perky's wife, Lucy, was sitting in the cool, leafy shade of the paperbarks with the baby in her arms and her five-year-old, Noel, clamped beside her. Noel was an engaging little fellow with his father's startling light blue eyes in a chocolate brown face. Lucy had been one of Bridie's girls at the homestead since her early teens. Toni knew her well, so she walked over to say hello and admire the baby and to talk to Noel, who was looking frustrated at being held by his mother. No doubt he wanted to sit on the fence, but it wasn't uncommon for brumbies to pose a threat.

While Lucy beamed with pleasure, Toni bent to speak to the baby, a plump little girl with her mother's huge liquid black eyes.

"Can I come sit with you, miss?" Noel cajoled, tugging on Toni's fingers.

"I told you, Noel," his mother warned.

"I wanna see Dad."

"You can see him well enough."

Toni relented. "I'll hold his hand, Lucy if that's all right with you. We'll stand beside the fence."

Lucy gazed at her son with love and wry amusement. "Just behave yourself, boy. I don't want nuthin' happening."

"Nothing will, Lucy," Toni assured her.

"It always does with Noel around." Lucy grinned.

"Mr. Beresford has been training Dad. He says he's a natural," Noel said proudly, trotting alongside Toni.

"I'm sure he is, Noel." Toni smiled, keeping a firm grip on the little boy's hand. "Knowing how to handle horses is a gift."

Byrne was still in the ring with the large, sleek, high-mettled colt. This was a horse that had never known bridle or hobbles. The silent, light-footed Perky, in his battered felt hat, denim shirt and jeans, red dust clogging his stockman's elastic-sided boots, turned to grin at his little son.

"Good on ya, Dad," the boy called. "Come on, Big Fella."

"Hush now." Toni bent over the boy. "You don't want to make the horse nervous, Noel. He's frightened enough already."

Just to prove it, Big Fella reared and began to bolt in a circle, kicking up the fine red dust, which rose in floating cloud castles. Perky swung a lasso and hung on tight, though the rope began to slip through his gloved hands.

"Come on," he said. "We won't hurt you. We're good pals, you and me."

"He's not ready to be pals, Perky," Joel hooted.

The sleek bay was digging in his heels, but Byrne moved closer, still gently swishing the bag, which began to engage the animal's curiosity. Finally he reached out to pat the horse's neck, gently, caressingly, his head inclined as he spoke to the horse with sympathy and affection. A lot of patting went on. A lot of crooning talk. Sweet whispering words that the horse responded to like magic. Byrne began long, gentle smoothing of the flanks, soothing the quivering brumby's muscles.

The bridle was over the horse's head. The bit went through the colt's soft open mouth. Without protest. The horse had never experienced anything like it before, a foreign object in its mouth, yet it started to chew on it rhythmically, much as Noel might have chewed on a hard caramel.

While Byrne continued to pat the animal, Perky slipped a halter over its head. The colt stood quite still, obviously wondering what was going to happen next. No threat was being offered. No pain. No fright. Byrne sank down, tied another rope to the halter and tossed it gently between the horse's legs where Perky looped it around a rear leg. With lots of words and pats, Big Fella was hobbled, miraculously quiet until it realised its legs were bound.

Then it totally bottomed out.

"Poor old fella. Poor old fella," Noel shouted, distressed.

Toni tried to explain to him. "It seems like that, but Big Fella has to be trained, Noel. Horses are very powerful. They can kick out, even kill. When Big Fella is broken in he'll make a good tough bush horse for your daddy to ride. He'll love his work."

One thing they could be sure of—Big Fella wasn't

liking what was happening now. He was screaming up a storm, charging then stumbling, the freedom of his gait inhibited by the hobbles. In the adjoining yard the other brumbies snorted and kicked in sympathy. Vigorous whinnies were exchanged.

"Don't wanna see no more," Noel cried, totally losing his smile.

"All right, pet." Contrite, Toni turned to take the boy to his mother. "Don't upset yourself. One day very soon Big Fella is going to make a fine ride. You have to go to school, don't you? Be taught."

"Waste of time," Noel said.

"You say that now because you miss being able to run around all day. But one day in the near future you're going to please everyone with all you've learned."

"Big Fella's a good horse," Noel said doggedly. "He should be able to play all day. Like *me*."

While Big Fella was being pushed into another holding yard, a look of astonishment on its face, Noel flopped into his mother's lap. "Don't like Big Fella tied up."

"We all gotta learn, son," his mother said. "It's pretty hard, losin' your natural spirit." Toni couldn't help but agree. Even humans were forced to conform.

Next into the ring was a slender, compact bronze-coloured horse with neck and head held high and the flash of fire in its eyes. Without the little boy to consider, Toni climbed onto the fence, taking a position in the shade some little distance from the others. With her fair skin she had to take extra care, and she didn't want her arms tanned to her shirt sleeves for the wedding.

For all its slenderness, the bronze horse showed strength and lightning quickness, circling the ring and evading Byrne's hand and that tricky burlap bag that seemed harmless but wasn't. There was magic in that rough waving cloth. Magic in the tall, powerful man with the soft, caressing voice.

The seductive wooing started again. They watched, entranced, as Byrne, with a wide variety of moves and soothing sounds, low whistles, clucks and whispering, slowly but surely gained the curious horse's confidence. This horse was going to be a good one. It wasn't until a good half hour later, when Perky took over from Byrne with one of the other aboriginal stockmen for an offsider, that Noel showed how difficult he was to restrain. While the others relaxed in the lull, Noel suddenly bounded from his mother's lap to join his father in the ring. He rolled like a top under the pole fence, startling everyone, including the spotted brumby in the ring.

It reared, standing high on its back legs. Then it began to charge.

Toni, closest to the child, acted without a minute's thought. She took a flying leap into the ring and grabbed the little boy by his shirt, though he was intent on evading her. Then, with all the swiftness and strength of frenzy, she started to propel them backward under the rail, the charge of adrenaline so great her ears were buzzing painfully.

The horse was bolting toward them, shaking the earth with the thunder of its hooves, until it was brought up by a lasso Byrne threw with great skill and precision. The backlash tore through his body. A hard grimace appeared on his face. Perky ran to him, latched onto the rope. Both men went over, tumbled, held, while the horse came to a shuddering stop against the rail, beaten and subdued.

"For God's sake!" Kerry reached his sister first, lifting the wailing little boy and handing him to his mother, who was shaking with reflex anger.

"You could have been killed, you little devil," Lucy sobbed.

Noel seemed to expect a cuff but got a violent hug instead.

Toni was lying on the ground, her eyes shut, her slender body in the fetal position, knees drawn up against her chest.

"Toni, you're all right, aren't you?" Kerry bent over her, appalled. He'd been certain she hadn't hurt herself. Now he wasn't sure.

"I've got grit in my eyes, damn it." She was breathing deeply, trying to get air in her lungs. She hadn't been scared for herself, there was no time, but she'd had a terrible vision of the little boy disfigured.

"At least you're in one piece." Kerry's voice wobbled in relief. "Maybe they ought to make you and Byrne a team on the circuit."

He broke off as Byrne strode toward them. Byrne all static electricity...

Fierce emotions were locked inside him. The incident, brief as it was, had struck him to the heart, like a hammer to an anvil. It also brought home how profound were his feelings. Fear was almost unknown to him, yet fear had engulfed him like a brushfire. For a split second he'd been rendered powerless. Powerless at a time when he needed all his strength and wits about him. The brumby had been desperate to break out of the enclosure. Desperate to protect itself against the people who kept it against its will. Desperate to lash out at anyone in its way. In that brief span of time he'd had to act. That was all he had. A split second. Too much emotion could paralyse, cause terrible tragedy. His father had impressed that on him from a very early age.

When he reached Toni he went down on his knees,

feeling some odd pain like the point of a knife at his heart. What did this terrible caring mean? Destruction of self? "Toni, are you hurt?"

"She could have been." Cate spoke through chattering teeth, though the cobalt air glittered with heat. "That was so *brave!*"

"I thought I made certain Lucy had charge of the boy. It's my fault," Byrne's voice rasped in his throat. "Children are so unpredictable."

"But she's all right," Kerry hastened to tell him, sensing Byrne's extreme tension. "So's little Noel, thank God."

"I've got grit in my eyes and I want something done about it now," Toni announced in such an irritated voice, Byrne reached for her and lifted her in his arms.

"Okay, I'll oblige. Keep your eyes shut tight. I'm going to take you down to the creek."

"Are you sure you aren't going to drown me?" She could feel the hard, corded muscles in his arms. Intuition told her he was upset and angry. At her. At Lucy. At himself.

"No, I'm going to duck your head under," he said tersely.

"Just dump me in. I don't care if I get wet."

"Neither do I." His laugh flared. Jangled, like him.

Next thing they were submerged beneath the jade green water, descending to a level that washed the grit from Toni's clenched eyes.

Eventually she opened them, saw silver specks on a fish that shot away from her. "Gosh, it's cold," she shouted, as they both broke the surface.

Byrne made no reply. He put his hands on her shoulders, taking them down again, the waters closing over their heads, into the dark green depths shot through here and there with golden rays, bursts of light against the eyes. One strong arm bound her to him while he pressed a deep, intoxicating kiss on her wet mouth. All in wonderful underwater slow motion.

The excitement of it was enormous. The calm waters might have become rapids. There was no chance of getting free. Not that she wanted to be free. Her heart was hammering wildly in her chest as his extraordinary force seemed to pass through her body, energising it. It was almost as though they shared a physical being, an intimacy that was astonishing to her.

"Don't ever frighten me again," he said when they surfaced. Silver droplets decorated his hair, clung to his black eyelashes, accentuating the dazzling beauty of his eyes.

At their expression exhilaration flashed through her. She felt lighter than air. She threw back her head and gave a sweet, joyous laugh. "When can I atone with a kiss?"

"We both know kisses can get out of control." He was shocked and aroused by a sudden vision of her beautiful naked body beneath him.

It was electrifying to be with him. An allurement she couldn't forgo. She loved this man. She loved him even as she knew his feelings were ambiguous. He prized his male autonomy. He guarded it so fiercely. She would have to find a sure way to reach him.

"Say, what's with you two?" Joel yelled from the bank.

"They sure as hell aren't fighting," Kerry said with a delighted laugh.

"I'd say *not*." Cate sounded thrilled.

"I'd say they were kissing." Andrea's expression was frozen.

Joel paid no attention to her at all. "Whatever Byrne wants, Byrne gets," he said with a mixture of resignation and admiration.

From the water Toni, graceful as a mermaid, lifted an arm. "Why don't you all join us?" she called. How beautiful the day! The blossoming trees! The prancing horses in the yard! Everything was glorious.

Her invitation raised a ready response. Joel looked at the others. "Why not? I'm all for celebrating life." He threw off his hat, tugged at his high riding boots then with wild yippee made a dash for the creek.

Without further ado Cate and Kerry went after him, whooping all the way, hitting the water together, laughing and splashing. The life force was deep within them as they surged together for a loving embrace.

Round the yard the stockmen broke into relieved laughter. Little Noel wanted to join them, but this time his father held him high in his arms. Only Andrea stood aloof, her love turned to hate.

It was true what they said, jealousy corroded the soul. Her worst fears were coming true. Byrne had succumbed to the Golden Girl's attraction, but the thought of it continuing was more than she could endure. Even at that moment he seemed to be enmeshed in her long gold hair. It fanned out like silk on the crystal clear water, both of them floating while Cate and the young men were sporting like dolphins.

Idiots! She hated them all. Or was it simply a high after a narrow escape? Was that the explanation? The girl had taken a considerable risk. She might look as delicate as a lily but she was swift and athletic, a beautiful, stylish rider. She should have taken into account that Toni Streeton had been born and bred on the land. Every moment the girl remained, Andrea felt her chances with Byrne slipping away. She had seen his eyes when he'd looked at the girl lying so still and vulnerable on the sand. The eyes told Andrea what she did not choose to know.

The freight plane arrived with supplies and a thick letter from Zoe.

"What has she got to say?" Kerry asked, as Toni stood on Nowra's veranda splitting open the envelope.

"Sit down and I'll read it out. Or would you like to read it yourself?"

Kerry looked at her gravely. "It's addressed to you, poppet."

"It's for both of us, I'm sure. I keep telling you, Zoe never lost her love for you."

"No, she just lost touch."

Toni winced, feeling a wave of pain pass over her. "*I* love you, Kerry," she said, her eyes blurred.

"I know you do," Kerry answered, his torment pushed aside.

"My dearest Antoinette," Toni began.

It was the start of a long, rambling letter full of anxiety, frustration, loneliness and all kinds of complaints. Zoe's romance wasn't going well. Though she used every bit of her charm, she wasn't getting on with Patrick's family, grown up and married, a whole network of them. The gap between herself and Patrick was widening. She had tremendous worries about her security. It was quite possible Claude, fed up, would write her off. She was missing Toni terribly. Having Toni around made life so much more stable. She had no one to do all her little tasks. No one to turn to for advice.

"Does she say anything at all about me? About the wedding?" Kerry asked in wonderment. "Or is it about

Zoe's trials and tribulations? Total self-absorption would sum her up.''

That struck Toni as particularly true. She leafed through another two pages, all related specifically to Zoe, finding on the last page the information that Zoe fully intended to fly home for ''her baby's'' wedding.

''I suppose I was pretty small when she left,'' Kerry said briskly.

''If you'd rather she didn't come, Kerry, I think I can persuade her.''

''I have to tell you, poppet, I'm full of conflict. I don't even understand myself.''

''It's the way we've lived.'' Toni sighed. ''Good or bad, mothers are the centre of family life. Zoe met none of our needs, yet we were all compelled to love her. We can't banish her from our lives or our minds.''

''No. I even wish I could look after her,'' Kerry admitted. ''You've taken enough on your shoulders.''

''I don't think Cate would like that. Or any of them, for that matter. The simple solution would be for Zoe to make a life for herself. Preferably with a good, strong, understanding man who couldn't be easily swayed.''

''And better yet has lots of money?'' Kerry asked with a rueful smile.

''I'm sure that's essential. Did I ever tell you Zoe is terrified of being poor? She's even more terrified of being poor than she is of growing old.''

''She lacks moral character.'' Kerry's expression was serious but not unkind.

''Well, she couldn't learn from good example. Her mother took off, and her grandmother, as well as being frugal, lacked a lot of the womanly virtues.''

''Why did she never tell me any of this?'' Kerry asked.

"You were openly disapproving of her, Kerry. Please don't mind my saying it. You believed loving Zoe was a sign of disloyalty to Dad. I know how much you looked up to him. Everyone did."

"You would have made a good psychiatrist," Kerry said, "but even you wouldn't know why he married her. She could never have measured up."

"They were *young!* The temptation, Kerry. She was so beautiful and she craved love and support. Dad would have been a pushover. Anyway, marriages are very complex affairs, as you'll find out yourself. Other people may have criticized our mother, but Dad never did. You know why? Because he loved her."

"I suppose. Anyway, it's wonderfully comforting to have you home. To sit down together to a good meal, a glass of wine, the table set so nicely, flowers and everything. I love having a woman about the place. Women are so *civilising.*"

Toni was alone at the homestead a few days later when Castle Hill's bright yellow helicopter landed on the front lawn. Kerry was away moving cattle. Toni didn't expect him until sundown. She had taken lunch out to him, stayed for a sandwich and a cup of tea, then returned to the house. She had a few programs in place—general tidying up, cleaning out cupboards, getting the place ready for Cate, everything done with an ache in her heart. So many reminders of her father! She intended to do some baking, as well. Kerry was particularly fond of her fruitcake, and she had planned a sirloin roast for dinner. Kerry needed a bit of fattening up before the wedding.

Quickly she took the cake from the oven, set it on the counter and covered it with a clean tea towel. It could cool in the pan. In the hallway she caught a glimpse of herself in the mirror. Long skeins of hair hung on either side of her cheeks, breaking away from the blue silk scarf she wore at her nape. Her cheeks burned with excitement. By the time she reached the veranda the helicopter rotors had slowed and Byrne was descending onto the lawn.

"Hi!" He lifted an arm. No smile. Just as well. The smile would have brought her undone.

"Is there a reason for this great honour?" she called, feigning a casual manner when she felt transcendent.

"No need to ask," he drawled, walking toward her with easy elegance that was a combination of perfect fitness, efficiency and natural grace. "I'm here to see *you*."

How did one fight those waves of charisma? Heat blended with the light inside her. "Heavenly! I thought you might be dropping some groceries off. Cate likes to make sure her beloved eats well."

"She can relax while you're here to look after him." He moved onto the veranda, studying her with such intensity she had to blink. If ever a man could make eye contact, he could.

"Come in," Toni invited as the excitement kept growing "Kerry's moving some cattle but he'll be back late afternoon."

"I know. I'm a cattleman myself," he told her laconically.

"I'm just making conversation."

"And cake, from that great aroma. It smells delicious. I might try some."

"You'll have to wait until it cools." She directed an uncertain glance at him, not sure if he was serious.

"You mean stay to dinner?"

She was filled with incredulous pleasure. "To tell the truth, that you'd want to stay never crossed my mind, but you'd be very welcome." She motioned him into the living room. "How's everyone?"

"Wondering what the hell's going on." He gave a vaguely discordant laugh.

"What do you mean?"

"Toni, you can't play dumb. You're a very smart girl."

"Ah, yes, but am I sensible, sober, trustworthy?" she asked dryly.

"Would you need to be, with your assets?"

"With *you* I would." Her body was stirring under his every glance, her nerves shivery with excitement.

"You do well in an emergency," he pointed out. Her courage had been exceptional.

"Anything else?"

"You're becoming one big problem." His tone was different as warring thoughts stirred.

"Why's that? Or don't you want to answer?"

"Sure. It's getting so I can't take my eyes off you."

"And you're used to keeping your distance?"

"Antoinette, I'm responsible for a lot of people's lives," he said.

"I know. What I don't know is why you think I compound your problems."

"You can see you might?" Attempts at evasion were long past.

"Why, are bad things going to happen?"

"Let's say we're too close." Perversely, attraction flowered more brilliantly each time they met.

"As in family?" she asked. "That's nonsense, and you know it. I think it's far more likely you'll never sell your soul to a woman."

He laughed again. She wasn't wrong. "No good could come of it. I keep thinking of the way I froze the other day."

For an instant Toni couldn't see a connection. Then she did. "You froze?" she said incredulously. "You moved with the speed of light."

"I'm not Superman." His expression was taut.

"Damned near. Perhaps too much responsibility has been thrust upon you. Ever think of that? Your father, like mine, died too soon."

His eyes narrowed, became hooded. "Are you analysing me? Really? I love it."

"I think I'm getting somewhere," she said gently.

"That bothers me all the more." And it did.

"Come and sit down," she said in a gentle, coaxing voice.

"Thanks. So why are you sitting way over there?" he asked when they were both seated in the living room.

"You're the one who warned me, Byrne. Where there's smoke, there's fire."

"So that much sank in." Unable to settle, he rose abruptly, all six-foot-three of him, with the prowling grace of a panther. "I don't want to sit around. I'm too damned restless. Make me a cup of coffee. I need to know if you're as domesticated as you're beautiful."

"A lot of women are both," she pointed out, trying to loosen her breath from its tight constriction. The tension was staggering.

"Cate tells me Zoe is definitely coming back."

"She says so, but I don't know if we can absolutely rely on it."

"We all learned that." As they moved into the hallway, he suddenly caught her around the waist. "Hello, Antoinette," he said in a dark, seductive voice.

"Hello, Byrne."

"Are you all mended now?" He drank her in, white gold hair, blue eyes.

"Almost better." Like a child, she turned her left elbow for his inspection. It had been grazed rather badly in her roll under the fence. "I want to be perfect for the wedding."

He never thought. It shocked him, the rush of sensual pleasure. He took her slender arm and lightly kissed the rapidly healing graze. She had skin like a baby, another thing to stimulate the senses that threatened to swamp him. He had become totally used to holding the power. Taken it for granted. "If I were someone else I'd be thinking of marriage proposals myself," he said, wryly.

"Don't be too sure I'd accept." Her tone was a mix of spirit and confusion.

"You'd do exactly what I say."

She stared into his brilliant, mesmerizing eyes. "Never!" Then she spoilt it by taking a ragged breath.

"Let's see." He seemed to consider. "Kiss me." It wasn't *entirely* gentle, the way he said it, but shivery.

A great wave of feeling overtook her. "Byrne, you scare me," she said truthfully.

His beautiful mouth twisted in derision. "You might as well know you scare me, too."

"And you don't like it. Byrne Beresford, who pushes buttons and everyone jumps."

He gave an exaggerated sigh. "It seems to have progressed to that stage, Antoinette. But I can never forget the job. It's a *big job*. A lifetime job. You can appreciate that. I don't have to spell it out."

"No." She looked down. "Attraction comes, attraction goes, but the job remains forever. What I don't understand is, what's the foundation for your mistrust of women?''

He took his time answering, studying her face intently. ''Early experience, maybe. It's not *all* women. It's *the* woman. The one who gets under my skin. Who gets in the way of my identity.''

She stood utterly still as though to move would threaten them both. ''You're an egotist, Byrne Beresford.'' She thought totally otherwise.

''Or I have a strong sense of my own survival. Males develop that early. You know why? We associate women with goddesses. Beings who can take a man to heaven or hell. It only takes one turn.''

''And me. What sort of woman am I supposed to be?'' Was she again being linked with her mother?

His silver-gray gaze seemed to look into her soul. ''You're beautiful. Loving, giving, vital, brave.''

''There has to be a down side.'' Already she was bracing herself for it.

He gave a short laugh. Lifted a long, sliding lock of her hair and put it over her shoulder, where it fanned into a gilded curtain. ''You're twenty-two years of age.''

''In addition to which, I'm Zoe's daughter?'' she challenged him quietly.

''Clearly Zoe couldn't ask for a more loyal daughter. No, Antoinette, I look at you as a person in your own right. Your character, your personality are unique to you.''

''Then you must have noticed I'm very bright for my age?'' She tried to smile.

''The brightest of all,'' he answered, his voice smoky with sensuality.

''And you, of course, are the one seducing me.''

At that he laughed, dancing lights in his eyes. "God, when I pray every night my self-control will prevail."

Toni let her gaze slip past him while she tried to say what was in her mind. He was playing her like a flute. "That may be your intention, but you send out two abundantly clear, conflicting messages, Byrne. One is, Come here to me. The other is, Don't encroach on my male space."

He gave a heart-stopping smile. Totally unfair. "Well, it just reveals my disordered frame of mind. Your fault, Antoinette. Having said that, you can stop trying to analyze me. What you really have to worry about is *this*."

The heat of his kiss seemed to peel her skin. There were no stages of response. Passion exploded like flame to gasoline. He pushed her head into the crook of his arm, a tall, strong man overpowering a slender young woman, delicate in comparison. No goddess in terms of control, but mortal woman dominated by a man's sensational primal sex drive.

Yet her body didn't resist him. It curved closer, like Leda curling to embrace the swan. There was no rational answer to the flame that ignited them, nor even some interacting chemical charge that mastered them. It was *magic*. A fantasy realm. For lovers alone.

She wanted him so badly she was facing total surrender to the mastery he could summon so effortlessly. He was crushing her, kissing her as though his tight control had fractured, threatening to split asunder, catching them both up.

When his hand sought her breast, she trembled like a sapling in the wind. The level of excitement was so high great bursts of heat radiated to all parts of her body, like a churning current overloading her veins. Such arousal demanded release. His hands were moving over her hips, defining the shape of her body, drawn impetuously, compulsively to her quivering core.

Where this would inevitably lead had already filtered into her overheated brain. She was leaving him in no doubt of her desperate need, but to be cast aside afterward would surely kill her. She knew she couldn't endure it. Desire was mutual. She could hardly fail to know that from the arousal of his hard, hungry body, the faint tremble in his powerful arms, but this was desire working on two levels. *She loved him.* She was absolutely connected to her feelings, openly expressing them, but his feelings weren't the same. Maybe he could never bring himself to put his heart into a woman's hands. Maybe he valued self-denial, if self-denial was necessary to protect his male supremacy. Yet he carried his passion into immediate action. Sweeping all before him.

"Byrne!" She had to gasp, partly out of excitement carried to extremes. She had almost added, *My love.* Her pride stopped her.

He held her very tight, his body molten. "I won't hurt you. I *can't* hurt you." But every time they came together he found it harder and harder to ride the rapids. The fact she responded to him so ravishingly beat up powerful waves of urgency. That fragrance on her skin. It was extraordinary. God, she was so sweet, incredibly endearing, a little shy of her own beautiful body. Slowly, very slowly, wishing to protect her, he got control of his caressing hands, fighting the almighty urge to carry her to her bedroom. It wasn't normal to him to put all considerations aside, but he almost had. It was a mark of his intense involvement. He drew back his head, staring into her rapt face. Her eyes were tightly closed and she was breathing through parted lips. The intensity of their lovemaking had robbed her of natural colour. She was as pale as porcelain.

"Open your eyes, Toni. *Please.*" He sounded shaken even to himself.

"I don't want to." For the first time in her life she was frightened of confronting reality. To look at him was to drown in a silver lake. "I feel as though you put me under a spell."

A sensation common to him. He couldn't deal with it, either. "From now on I think we oughtn't to be alone."

"I think you may be right." She gave a little trembly laugh and permitted her eyes to open on his marvelous face.

She didn't know it, but her arousal was such the pupils of her eyes, the focus of her face, had invaded the violet-blue irises. "Now we know how strong our feelings are, we'll have to work at keeping them under control," he said a little harshly.

"I don't see it as easy!" Her breath fluttered in her throat.

"No." He felt as protective of her as when she had surprised and delighted him as a little girl with her beauty and charm. "I'm sure you have a very nice bed," he said with something close to self-mockery, "but what do you say to a spin in the helicopter? We need a diversion. I'll take it out over the desert."

Where he led, she had to follow. "I'd like that, Byrne. If you give me a moment to catch my breath and maybe change out of this dress."

He looked at her. Springtime in a gauzy low-necked flower-patterned dress that revealed her peaking breasts.

His mouth twisted. "You'd look lovely in an old burlap bag." Her beauty wasn't made up of lighting, of makeup, of colour, it was simply there. *Absolute.*

CHAPTER SIX

FLYING over the desert, Toni remembered trying to explain to one of her French friends, who held the traditional concept of a desert as a Sahara of shifting sand quite devoid of vegetation, what *her* desert home was like. The Australian desert landscape was quite different to anywhere else on earth. There were sand hills to the horizon, but equally there were ancient colourful ranges, splendid gorges, flat-topped mesas and awe-inspiring monolithic rocks presiding over vast spinifex plains and mulga flats with their diversity of vegetation. And in the depths of the gorges, water. Precious water. Here permanent pools were the fabled oases, the jade green water surrounded by lush rainforest growth—white-barked, green-foliaged gums, palms and pandanus, a profusion of ferns and mosses and orchidlike lilies. These were places that stole the breath away with their unexpectedness. This was the driest continent on earth, but an island, which permitted rain to reach the so-called Dead Heart from any direction. The phenomenal transformation of the desert after rain held them all in awe each time it appeared, the brief glory as uplifting and indelible as a deep spiritual experience, an affirmation of the survival of man, of the land, of the soul.

Even the glittering gibber plains had an enormous fascination. Here not even the millions of paper daisies, the everlastings, could encroach on the gibber stone desert they were flying over. Since time immemorial the ground was completely covered by stones of all shapes and sizes. The windblown sands had polished them to such a high degree they resembled glossy gemstones, reflecting the brilliant fire of opals, black opals, milk opals, the polished white quartz helping to create the effect of some wonderful mosaic laid down by the Creator. In the distance lay an eroded range, its bright raw earth colours beginning to turn violet as the atmospheric haze increased. The Outback was famous for its daily pageant of changing colour, a display Toni had sorely missed all the time she had been away.

"Seen enough?" Byrne called when they had been airborne some time.

"I'll never see enough." She raised her voice above the sound of the whirring rotors. "This is my country, Byrne. Every bit as much as it's yours."

He looked at her, smiled, his dark face full of approval.

When they were flying back Toni caught a glitter of light like a laser beam from the vast, empty land below them.

That's odd. Very odd, she thought, touching Byrne's arm and pointing to the sun-baked earth. "A beam of light."

"I see it." He was instantly, sharply alert. "A dog, as well. A cattle dog. No dingo."

The dog was racing in circles, obviously trying to attract attention, a comment on the dog's intelligence.

"We'll go down. Take a look," Byrne mouthed.

Nearing the ground, they caught sight of a battered four-wheel drive, the chassis coated thickly with the all-pervading red dust. There was no sign of life from the vehicle, which appeared to be half tipped into a depression beside a small stand of gnarled mulgas, one dead skeleton stark black against the blue, cloudless sky.

The dog had ceased its frantic circling, staring at the helicopter as it began its descent.

"Stay here," Byrne ordered when they set down, turning to leave her.

She wasn't about to disobey. Not a month went by without some tourist getting into serious trouble trying to explore the desert, not a friendly environment. Incidents flashed through Byrne's mind, desert tragedies. It struck him forcibly this could be another. He felt the man's presence before he saw him, lying on his side close to a sparse thicket of underbrush. Byrne moved to him quickly, speaking words of encouragement as he went. The survivor was maybe in his early sixties with silver hair tied back in a ponytail, and had that sadly shrunken appearance of the badly dehydrated, his skin red and shiny with sunburn.

"How's it going?" Byrne went down on his haunches, taking the man's wrist and feeling for his pulse. Slow.

"My nephew." The man swallowed hoarsely, trying to raise his head. It fell back. "He's gone ahead to see if he could get help."

Byrne was already standing, keeping any sharp comment to himself. No matter how many warnings were posted, too few heeded what was a life-and-death warning. *Don't on any account leave your vehicle.*

He limited himself to a quiet comment. "Hang in there, I'll bring water and the first aid kit. Then I'll track down your nephew. How long has he been gone?"

The man shook his head painfully, having lost all sense of time.

Byrne bent, touched his arm. "Try not to worry. He should be easy to spot from the air."

He ran to the helicopter, his dark copper skin sheened with sweat by the time he reached it. Toni was already at the door opening, the first aid kit and a canteen of water to hand.

"A survivor?" she asked carefully when Byrne was near. The fact he was running gave her hope.

Byrne removed his Akubra, raked back his dark hair. "Elderly chap. In a bad way. He can't tell me much. There's a nephew. He's gone on ahead."

"Ahead where?" Toni asked in dismay. Her stomach twisted at the prospect they might have to deal with a dead man.

Byrne declined to answer. He took her hand while she jumped to the ground. "No one listens. That's the incredible thing."

"So what do you want me to do?" Toni asked briskly, her energy flowing in the emergency.

"Can you take charge of the guy?" he asked, reluctant to leave her but with no other option.

"Sure I can," she said competently, shading her eyes against the heat.

"I may not be able to get back to you for some time, okay? He might be huddled up somewhere, camouflaged. I'll have to fly low."

"You'll find him," Toni said with confidence. "I just pray he's alive."

"You and me both." Byrne took a harsh intake of breath. "I'll come with you to the man's side. Explain who you are." *My girl,* he thought like some abrupt revelation. *My woman.* He damned near said, "I love you."

"What about the small tarpaulin over the back," she asked, unaware of the thoughts that electrified him.

He reached in to get it. "You know what to do with the water?"

"Of course. Little sips at first." She stood at his shoulder.

"I'll get away as soon as possible. There isn't a moment to be lost."

Attuned to him, she laid her hand on his arm, knowing how fragile life was. "Take care, Byrne."

His eyes seemed to blaze in his dark face. He bent, dropped a brief kiss on her mouth that tingled to her toes. "I'll be back for you. Never fear."

It was better with the tarpaulin spread like a canopy across the small thicket. The man—he told her his name was John Courtney, "a foolish old academic"—lay more comfortably on his side, his head propped on a makeshift pillow. Toni held his hand. Clearly it gave him comfort. He had a daughter, he told her. Grandchildren. Water had revived him. Toni marvelled as always at its extraordinary effect. It was like the miracle of the living desert. Instant survival. The man's body, thin but previously in good shape, was raw with sunburn, and there were multiple scratches all over the backs of his hands. He didn't know how he got them.

Toni didn't encourage him to talk but contented herself with quiet words of comfort and encouragement. The dog, Bluey, was their loyal companion, sitting beside Toni as though he had mysteriously chosen her as their leader. That or the intelligent animal was extremely grateful for the drink of water she had poured into a makeshift plastic container. The dog was in a lot better condition than his travelling companion. Toni suspected he had been getting moisture from the purple parakeelya, a succulent the cattle herds were able to feed on. Her long hair was soaked with sweat. It lay in a thick, heavy plait on her nape. Sweat ran between her breasts and trickled down her legs. She would have given anything for a breeze, but the next best thing was a wet washcloth and a controlled flow of water from the canteen. Once John Courtney mumbled, and his hand went slack, causing Toni's stomach to lurch. She feared he could suffer a heart attack or stroke. She had no real idea of his condition. She put her head down and prayed for Byrne's return.

He found the exhausted young man in a dry gully almost hidden from sight by the great rings of spinifex, each plant some ten feet across and nearly three feet high. It reminded him of how wallaroos, the large kangaroos, used the rings as windbreaks when they wanted to take a quiet nap. Maybe the young fellow had heard about it and thought to take shelter.

Like his uncle, though separated by a good thirty years, the nephew was badly sunburned, dehydrated and in a state of exhaustion. Byrne attended to him as best he could, then, when the patient had difficulty walking, carried the young man to the helicopter, where he bundled him in. In times like this, he blessed his strength and fitness. He had made radio contact with the Flying Doctor Service, giving an exact location for the rescue. Both men needed urgent medical attention. The service's Cessna would make short work of getting to the site then to Base Hospital.

He was worried about Toni. He knew in this heat the time would go very slowly while she waited for him to get back. He thought of her beautiful skin, protected by little more than a wide-brimmed hat and the edge of the tarpaulin. He threw himself into the pilot's seat. The engine caught, the rotors whirred. They were lifting almost vertically through the exquisite silver lines of mirage into the cobalt air. He glanced at the young man who was already drooping in his seat and pushed him back.

"All right," he urged himself sharply. "Let's go."

There was a doctor and a nurse on board the Cessna, a married couple Byrne knew well. The two men made short work of getting the badly dehydrated survivors into the plane.

"The young fellow will pull through, no question," the doctor told them quietly. "The older man doesn't look good. The sooner we get him to the hospital the better. It was a miracle you spotted them. As I see it they wouldn't have survived another day."

"I'll call tonight, Bill. Check on their progress," Byrne said.

"Fine. Where would they be but for you? How intelligent men can set out without sufficient food or water, without telling anyone where they're going..."

"It happens all the time," Byrne commented briefly.

"Well, it was close. Exceptionally close."

They stood watching the aircraft take off with Bluey, left in their care, wagging his tail beside them, keeping the plane in sight until it disappeared over the larkspur range.

Byrne turned, took Toni by the shoulders and stared into her heat-flushed face. "You did very well, Antoinette."

She'd have crawled on her hands and knees for the look in his eyes. "You were the real saviour. I didn't do much at all. Just offered a bit of comfort."

"Whatever you did, Courtney's convinced you're an angel. An angel come from heaven to lend aid."

"It's the blue eyes and blond hair." She smiled.

"Sure." He sounded impressed. "We can take that into account, but it doesn't give credit to the depth of your soul. If one has to share a life-and-death experience it ought to be with an angel, don't you think?" He spoke lightly, but there was intense feeling in his eyes.

"I'm mortal, Byrne, with all a mortal's frailties." Utterly absorbed, neither of them seemed conscious of the searing heat.

"Still, Courtney blessed you. So do I."

Silently he took her face between his hands, his gaze centring on her full, lovely mouth. There was such a burning inside him. He was growing accustomed to it. As much as he had tried to harden his heart against her, one glance from her violet eyes undermined the whole senseless process.

"You're not what I expected, Antoinette," he said softly. "In fact I'm losing day to day."

She was totally rapt in his aura. "I'm just one woman, Byrne."

He almost laughed. One woman who given so little time almost held him in the palm of her hand. God, what had befallen him? Did she *know?* "I'm glad you came." Just watching her melted his heart.

"And this is where I'm staying."

She might have meant within his arms. His smile dropped away. His breathing changed. He was craving to kiss her, crush her. Did she recognise it? In one swift, blinding motion he folded her against him, his desire soaring as her tender mouth parted while his bore downward. Her lips were ineffably soft, like rose petals, yet they brought his passion to a peak in a way he had never thought possible. He gripped her slender back, her narrow waist, his nostrils filling with the fragrance of her wonderful satin skin. The kiss seemed to go on forever, but he knew it had to stop, and the sun's rays were concentrated on them, so powerfully hot Byrne drew a deep, reluctant breath.

"Now you understand how weak you've made me."

She was astonished by the little lick of self-derision, as though he was somehow violating his own codes. "You're wrong," she protested. "You're so strong. You have no need to fear me."

His beautiful mouth twisted. "Accept it, sweetheart. I do. A slip of a girl to breach my defenses." He turned and whistled for Bluey, who had been looking at them in a bright, inquiring fashion, head cocked. "Come on, boy. It's your turn to get a bit of attention."

The survivors took several days to recover from their experience in the desert, and Byrne kept Toni informed of their progress. Later, John Courtney wrote her a wonderful letter that brought tears to her eyes. Even in the hospital he had praised her to the heavens when Toni had thought in his sorry condition he had barely registered her presence. Not so.

"Take a pat on the back," Kerry advised her. "You deserve it."

Kerry's stag party was coming up. A night in town, and afterward he arrived home with a crew cut.

Toni looked at him in dismay. "Oh, Kerry. What fool did that?"

Gone were the waves, the brown highlighted with golden streaks. In its place a style reminiscent of Bruce Willis at his toughest. "If you must know it was P.J., and a couple of his mates held me down." Kerry gave her a carefree grin, apparently not disturbed at all.

"Idiots! Where was Byrne? He wouldn't have let this happen. Cate wants a handsome bridegroom with a full head of hair."

"It doesn't look that bad, does it?" For the first time Kerry sounded shamed and anxious. In fact, he still looked very attractive. "Byrne wasn't there at the time. I think he got tired of our antics. I know he gave Joel a blast later. Don't worry, poppet, it will grow. It was too long, anyway. Even you said that. And I have to tell you it's cool." He took his sister in his arms and hugged her.

When Cate saw her beloved she wasn't as upset as Toni had predicted. "It could have been worse," she said laconically. "They could have shaved the whole lot off or do what they did to Andy Gilmore. When he passed out they put his leg in plaster and told him he broke it. Anyway, it makes him look rather macho. Shows off his good bones."

Toni shook her head in wonderment.

Cate's party was held in town, girls only. It turned out a far more commendable affair. Cate was a very popular young woman, and her friends came from all over to fete her and wish her well. Eight days to the wedding, and the presents had begun to arrive by the planeload, everything a young couple could possibly want, all of it set out in the library on long makeshift tables covered with green damask to show off the gifts.

Kerry and Toni walked up and down admiring the highest quality silver, crystal, the dinner sets of various makes and designs, the vases and clocks, a vast array of ornaments, blankets, bedspreads and quilts, fine sheets and exquisite table linen. There were rugs, modern and antique, luggage, glasses galore. There was even some wonderful-looking garden furniture and a life-size statue of a woodland nymph.

"We won't have to buy anything for a very long time," Kerry said in amazement.

"If you even get around to unpacking it." Toni smiled.

Toni's present to them was a pair of sterling silver salts standing some three inches high, the sides decorated with sprigs of flowers and leaves and set with three gleaming opals, part of a collection her father had started for her when she was a child. She had commissioned the work in Paris, and the young designer, charmed by the idea, had put his heart and soul into the work, a decorative as well as functional object.

Cate had accepted the gift with tears in her eyes. "They're absolutely beautiful, Toni. We'll use them all the time."

"Thanks, poppet." Kerry bent to kiss her. "I know what those opals mean to you."

It was Kerry who raised the subject of Byrne. Toni had been more or less expecting it when their every encounter, supposedly so casual, shook the air. Brother and sister were relaxing after dinner, coffee in hand, when Kerry suddenly demanded, "What's with you and Byrne? I don't think I can take another day of suspense."

"Same here." Toni gave a deep, laconic sigh. "I'm madly in love with him."

Kerry chortled. "I hate to tell you this, kiddo. You always were."

"Maybe it was the way he used to treat me. The young, lordly, knock 'em dead handsome Byrne Beresford, heir to the Beresford chain and fortune, used to make my thirteen-year-old heart melt. He told me I used to remind him of a Persian kitten."

"I can see that," Kerry said. "Even to your brother you were adorable."

"Except he doesn't *want* to love me, Kerry."

Kerry considered, his brows coming together. "You mean he's fighting the big attraction?"

"For all he's worth," Toni answered with feeling.

"He's a complex character." Kerry looked at her. "He plays his own game, if you know what I mean. He's like a feudal baron. He almost can be, in our part of the world. He's absolutely central to the whole Beresford clan's interests. God, he's not even thirty-two but he's been running things for years. It's a big responsibility and it takes its toll. He can't ever be free of problems, anxieties. As far as I'm concerned it's too much to handle. Everything about him, his habits, his gestures, his movements, his speech. He's so damned self-reliant. Maybe it's reached painful and powerful proportions."

"You mean he has to face he's human after all?" Toni asked wryly. "He sees falling in love as a weakness?"

"More likely he can't easily tolerate loss of control. His father was so tough on him, expected so much, it was kind of dehumanising. Maybe that's a bit extreme."

"No, I know what you mean. Byrne was the ideal son. The ultimate self-reliant man, as it should be if he was going to be given so much money and power. But no one, absolutely no one can alienate him from his passionate nature. And he does have one."

"Hell, you think I don't know that?" Kerry tossed a Belgian chocolate paper aside. "Byrne has a lot of emotion dammed up inside him. I've said all along. He's passionate about everything he does. How he handles his responsibilities. They all simply leave everything to him. Beside him Joel's a playboy."

"He'll learn," Toni said equably. "Maybe Joel was the lucky one. He lived outside his father's main sphere of interest. Cate, too. Even as a child I realised Byrne was everything. The chosen one."

"And along came Antoinette Streeton."

"The last thing I expected, Kerry, was for Byrne to look at me. I was a child when he was the young master of all he surveyed. I really believe he would have liked me to remain a child."

"Hardly possible, kiddo." Kerry laughed. "Give him time. This is a new kind of relationship for Byrne."

"What about Andrea Benton?" Toni looked up to gauge Kerry's reaction.

He paused to consider. "Andrea was doing all the running. Byrne's no monk. Women fling themselves at him. You know that. He's everyone's hero. Dazzlingly handsome, and all that money. Come to that, the girls don't leave Joel alone, either. Take Fern. She's hanging in there for all she's worth. Pushing it, if you ask me. A female's instinct is to land a man from the cradle."

"Without a doubt, but not *a* man. *The* man." Toni sighed. "I think Byrne's responses are tempered by the fact he's known me since I was a baby. And I'm Zoe's daughter.''

"You mean intrinsically flighty?" Kerry's relaxed expression tightened.

"That's too severe, but having such a mother might be a factor. Byrne has a set of requirements that might be very hard to live up to. Also, I think he's feeling a bit guilty at having his old friendly feelings abruptly translated into desire. In addition to which we're almost family.''

Kerry rocked back in his chair so impetuously he almost threw himself off balance. "Oh, hell, Toni, cut it out. Maybe falling so hard is just too difficult for Byrne to deal with. His self-image is keeping control and so forth. You may be younger, but you're plenty mature. Think positive, girl.''

Toni had to smile. "Thanks, brother, I will." She reached for the coffeepot and filled their cups. "There's another thing we should discuss now the wedding is on us.''

"Nowra?" Kerry's voice was anxious.

"You don't think Cate should buy out my share?" Toni suggested.

"You think that's a good idea?"

"She's an heiress, Kerry. Nowra will be home. I don't want Byrne to do it.''

"No. I can understand that. It is a funny feeling knowing they can buy and sell us a hundred times over. But Cate..." Kerry shook his head. "I don't want to use her money.''

"She'll be your wife, Kerry."

"I can't feel exactly happy about it."

"I don't feel happy about selling, either. Dad is here

at this place. I can get in touch with him just sitting in his study or riding through the bush, taking the trails we used to take together. I loved him so much.'' Unexpectedly Toni burst into tears, and immediately Kerry shoved back his chair, going down on his haunches and cradling her head to his chest.

''Hey, don't cry. Dad adored you, poppet. His little princess. He hated your going away, but he knew you wanted time with Zoe. Two females, I guess. Women stick together.''

Toni lifted her head, tried to smile. ''What are you going to do when Zoe comes home?''

''*If* she comes home,'' Kerry said. ''When could I ever depend on Zoe?''

''Try not to condemn her, Kerry,'' Toni begged. ''You're her only son. She loves you.''

Kerry rose to his feet. ''I can do without that sort of love. I have Cate and you. I'm never going to be on my own again.''

Four days before the wedding Zoe arrived in Australia via Bangkok. Very generously Byrne flew brother and sister to meet her at the domestic terminal. Cate came along to lend her fiancé moral support. Toni felt, not for the first time, that Cate was going to make a very good mother. She loved mothering Kerry.

Zoe's flight came in right on time. She had spent the night in Brisbane, the state capital, before continuing her journey. Because it was a country terminal, they were able to see her as she descended the gangplank, her beautiful blond hair catching all the rays of the sun. From a distance she looked like Toni's sister.

''I can't believe it,'' Kerry moaned. ''I'm so damned

nervous.'' He had been endlessly rearranging the collar of his shirt and rubbing the knees of his jeans all the time they had been waiting.

''No need, Kerry.'' Cate took his hand for comfort. ''This is your mother, and lordy, doesn't she look glamorous.''

Zoe indeed was an uncommonly beautiful woman. She lit up the space around her. People turned their heads to stare. Not only was she beautiful, she had enormous chic, bringing to a blue silk shirt and colour-matched linen slacks a marvelous elegance.

''So she finally made it,'' Byrne said with an appreciative smile.

''Thank God. I'm so pleased.'' Toni's face showed her relief and excitement. Kerry had had it firmly entrenched in his mind their mother didn't really care about him, that she wouldn't come home for his wedding. But there she was! Toni flew to her, was caught, held tight, kissed Euro style on both cheeks.

''My darling, my darling,'' Zoe exclaimed, like a born Parisian slipping into a second tongue. ''Where is my baby, where is my Kerry?'' She looked toward the little group. ''Mon Dieu, is that Byrne? What a fabulous-looking man.''

It wouldn't have been Zoe if she hadn't noticed. Kerry, however, was trying desperately not to be so self-conscious. He felt about ten years old, loving his mother so much but trying not to be embarrassed by her behaviour.

''Go to her, Kerry,'' Cate urged, almost but not quite pushing him.

She, too, felt upset. What was Zoe's arrival going to mean? Reconciliation, which she knew in her heart

Kerry wanted, or a kind of instant chaos? Zoe was that sort of person.

Toni was looking towards her brother, trying by sheer force of will to direct him into his mother's arms, while Zoe herself was starting to look faintly troubled.

"Take control, Kerry," Byrne directed. "This is for the best."

Immediately Kerry broke away from them, going toward his mother, who lifted her arms to him with such grace a man who had been watching her bumped into a pillar.

Cate had to look away, her eyes filled with tears, but Byrne continued to study the family tableau. Zoe was the source of Toni's extraordinary beauty. No question of that. But Toni was so much besides. It was she who calmed mother and son, bringing them into each other's arms.

Toni was so steadfast, so absolutely loyal. It was a quality he admired.

"It's all right. You can look now," Byrne murmured gently in his sister's ear. "Zoe's not going to cause any awkwardness. Toni will see to it. She'll make things right."

For all of that first day and evening, Zoe walked around saying how quiet it was. "I can hear my own heart pumping."

"It's not really all that quiet," Kerry said with a grin. "There are always the birds."

"People simply don't realise our quality of silence," Zoe said. "People in the cities. It's *extraordinary*. I've almost forgotten how extraordinary. But I haven't forgotten the house. Sometimes it used to annoy me the way your father wouldn't let me do it up. I could do anything else. You've done the best you can with it, Toni, darling. I can see your graceful hand. I expect Cate has lots of ideas, Kerry?" Zoe looked at her son out of her big blue eyes. "Such a fine girl. She takes after Sonia in looks. But that Byrne! He's something else! If he moved into my world the women wouldn't give him a minute's peace. He's as handsome as any film star. The same smoldering excitement. Is he involved with anyone?"

"He seems to have taken a fancy to Toni," Kerry said, shooting his sister a wry look.

"And not sure if he's liking it," Toni said.

Zoe looked dismayed. "I hope it doesn't have anything to do with me. I always found the Beresfords so judgmental. Sonia especially. Maybe my daughter mightn't seem good enough for her splendid son."

"She doesn't have any objections to me," Kerry pointed out mildly.

"You look like your father, darling. It's that simple. Your father never judged me. He remained my dearest friend."

"Which was why you never came back?" Kerry laughed shortly.

"I was too far away, Kerry," Zoe said in a quiet, serious voice. "I've suffered for it. So has Toni, who was blameless. I'm praying you're going to forgive me."

Kerry, who had been sitting on the edge of the table, stood up. "I forgive you, Mamma," he said, realising at some point he had, "but I'll never understand."

"You might one day, darling, when you have more experience of life. Many things don't go as we plan. Is there more coffee, Toni?" she asked brightly, changing the subject. "I'm addicted to coffee. *Good coffee.* We'll have to get some in. I must show you my outfit later. Francine worked very hard on it. Claude bought me a beautiful necklace and earrings to go with it. A sort of parting gift. We had a long, long talk. He always did act the father figure. He's been very generous. Very generous, indeed. I won't want for anything for the rest of my life.''

"Good Lord! Not even another husband?" Kerry couldn't resist it.

"I'm a woman who doesn't like being on her own, my darling." Zoe was entirely unoffended. "I have to have a man around."

Zoe rested all the following afternoon in preparation for the prewedding dinner at Castle Hill.

"It's absurd, you know, but I have butterflies in my tum," she told Toni as she finished her dressing.

"It will all work out," Toni soothed her. "You look lovely." Zoe was wearing her blond hair in a new short style. It was very natural and youthful, and it revealed the grace of her neck.

Zoe turned to get a sideways view of her elegant St. Laurent suit in a rich cream. "In this old thing?"

"I've never seen it before," Toni said dryly.

"Oh, well, it is *fairly* new. I've lost a little weight. Have you noticed?"

"You're a pocket Venus. Of course you've been through a lot. Losing Patrick, saying goodbye to poor old Claude and all," Toni teased.

"My problem is I'm just too damned lovable," Zoe explained, apparently quite seriously. "I thought the breakup with Claude was going to be a disaster, but it all turned out to be wonderfully friendly."

"You mean because he made you a generous settlement?"

"Claude gave me money because I *need* it, darling."

Toni had a sudden brain wave. "What if Kerry wanted to borrow some?"

Zoe put down her hairbrush and looked at her daughter warily. "What are you talking about, darling?"

"I suppose it all depends on what Claude gave you."

"A lot!" Zoe looked both grateful and triumphant. "'You've got to take it, Zoe,' he said to me. 'I can't bear to think of you going from husband to husband. I want to make you independent.' Incidentally he's a lot richer than I thought."

"Of course. He was too smart to tell you. You mightn't like this, Zoe, but there's the question of my share of Nowra."

Zoe stared at her, then laughed lightly. "Surely Byrne will buy you out? The Beresfords are absolutely loaded."

"I don't want that, Mamma."

"Lord, darling, you don't want *me* to take it on?" Zoe asked in wide-eyed astonishment. "What's the property worth these days? Do you know?"

"We can find out. You owe Kerry."

"Lord, don't I know it." Zoe sighed deeply and sank onto the bed, supple as a cat. "I can see how I've hurt him."

"You've got the opportunity to make amends. I'll sell out to you for way below what my share is worth. You give my share to Kerry as a wedding present. That way Nowra stays with the Streetons. *Our* family."

Zoe stared at her. "It's a big thing, darling," she finally burst out. "You'd be the loser. I'll be rich, but I can't throw money away, mind you."

"This is your big chance, Mamma. You could announce it tonight."

Zoe's blue eyes, bright as sapphires, suddenly began to glitter. "I think I'd enjoy that. Tell me about Sonia. Is she as uppity as ever?"

"She means well." Toni smiled.

"Darling, you know perfectly well she's very high-handed."

"You and she are going to share grandchildren, Mamma."

Zoe, in the act of smoothing her short straight skirt, looked uncertain. "Look at me, darling. Do I look like a grandmother?"

Toni reached out, caught her mother's hand and gave it a little shake. "I think when the time comes, Mamma, you're going to come into your own."

CHAPTER SEVEN

THE family dinner went off very well. Everyone around the table was on their best behaviour, each determined to stand united to hold onto the magic that was starting to make the air sparkle. This was going to be the perfect wedding. Who could doubt it? Look at the young couple. They were blissfully happy. Sonia had seemed momentarily stunned by Zoe's ageless appearance when they arrived but quickly recovered to play the gracious hostess and mother of the bride. Even Zoe managed to curb her natural flirtatiousness by not directing it at Byrne, so charming, so courteous, so devastatingly handsome. He appealed to her enormously, but his glittering silver-gray eyes were always turned toward Toni. Not that Toni didn't look ravishing, Zoe thought proudly, wishing for something she couldn't possibly have back. Youth. *What it is to be young!* she thought. She hadn't really experienced the shining, carefree days of youth. Perhaps that was what was the matter with her. She had married too early. She had married too *often.* She saw it all now. She had never met Mr. Right. She had met a lot of villains. Except Eric and Claude.

Zoe waited until the end of dinner before she made her announcement.

"My dear friends," she began in her captivating voice, "Cate, my daughter-in-law-to-be, my children, I want you to know nothing could have stopped me from coming home to attend this wonderful wedding, the uniting of our two families. It gives me great joy, as I know it would have Eric. I've thought long and hard about my wedding present to you, Kerry and Cate." Zoe paused to beam at them, happiness and triumph in her beautiful eyes. "And I have decided to give you Nowra in its entirety. Naturally I will compensate my daughter for her share. It's what we both want, and I hope it makes you happy."

Amazement all around. Delighted exclamations.

All the time Zoe was talking, Byrne was studying Toni intently. He could see her hand in this. For Toni it would be the perfect solution. He knew she didn't want to be beholden to him or have her brother beholden to him, either. She had the same stiff-necked pride as her father. He liked it. He wondered what she had said to Zoe. He wondered how Zoe would be able to come up with the money. He knew she had married three rich men, each richer than the last. Obviously, for all her talk of dwindling resources, she still had a sizable nest egg, or the long suffering Claude had given her a very generous settlement. If so, Claude had to be some kind of saint.

Afterward Zoe was taken to see the huge array of wedding presents, none of which could possibly outshine her own, then the adjoining ballroom where the wedding ceremony would be held. Tomorrow the decorators would be flown in, along with the floral designer and his staff, all of whom, thrilled with the prospect of handling a big society wedding, had visited the homestead some months earlier to formulate plans. The great wealth of flowers—roses, lilies, carnations, orchids, great sheaves of the pure white gladioli "The Bride", bearded iris in all the whites, rose pinks, lilacs and violet blues,

Singapore orchids, hyacinths, delphiniums, clouds of baby breath, a great array of greenery and ferns, stacks of glossy camellia leaves and the sweetly perfumed lily of the valley and stephanotis—would be held in one of the refrigerated rooms, along with crates and crates of champagne and the mountains of delectable food that would be turned into a wonderful feast by the caterers.

The countdown had begun. From now on Castle Hill would be a hive of activity as everyone went into top gear. A large family contingent was due on the morrow, with two of the groomsmen and the three little flower girls among the party. Many guests were sharing private and charter flights, and many more were making the trek overland or had already found lodgings in the nearest township of Beresford. The dormitories and bungalows had been taken over for the use of the guests, and the station staff temporarily relocated. A lot of the staff had been taken off their normal duties to help around the grounds, the gardens fed by underground bore water and coaxed to perfection, in the homestead and at the old stone stables complex, recently transformed into a marvellously memorable great function room with kitchen facilities a top hotel might envy. No expense had been spared to make the historic complex a splendid venue for the wedding. A string quartet had been engaged for the ceremony, a young cousin with an angelic boy soprano voice would sing three of the bride's favourite wedding songs, and a well-known band had jumped at the opportunity to play at the reception. A top videographer was flying in, as well as a young woman who was making quite a name for herself as a beautiful creative photographer. Every base was covered.

Cate's theme, mating swans, had been worked into

wonderfully natural topiary. There would be classical floral arrangements for the entrance hall and the central staircase, ballroom and the hall. There would be a magnificent ice sculpture for the table. Even the four-tier wedding cake, executed by a firm specialising in imaginative design, had incorporated the swan theme. Large antique silver swans, family heirlooms, would hold dozens of closely packed white roses on the bridal table. Cate even had the swan motif embroidered into her lingerie. Swans mated forever. That was what she wanted of her marriage. For it to last forever.

With everything so meticulously planned, Cate sailed through her days relaxed and happy, apparently without stress, while Kerry unexpectedly found himself prey to anxieties. Much as he loved Cate and longed to make her his wife, he was extremely aware of the great step they were taking. A child of divorce, he looked on his marriage vows as sacred. He began to feel an exaggerated concern he mightn't be good enough for his precious Cate, who was intrinsically a very balanced and happy person, unlike himself.

"Prewedding jitters." Zoe laughed the whole thing off. "Usually reserved for the bride."

Zoe would know.

Toni, on the other hand, took her brother's concerns seriously. Kerry always had been sensitive.

"I love her so much, I couldn't bear to let her down," Kerry confided.

"I understand that, Kerry. It means you truly love her. But you have to give yourself a break, let your nerves settle. Listen to your heart. It's going to be your perfect day. As wonderful as you've ever dreamed. You don't want to spoil that, do you?"

"Of course not." Kerry's brown eyes softened with affection.

"So relax and let go." Toni pulled him up by the arm. "And just to help you along, I'll make us a cup of tea."

"Thanks, Toni." He smiled.

In a never-ending succession of brilliantly fine days, the morning of the wedding dawned with a light shower. The birds were ecstatic, and every man, woman and child on the station took it as a good omen. The ceremony to be performed by Bishop John McGrath, who had baptised all Sonia's children and Zoe's, was scheduled for four o'clock, when the western sky would begin its marvellous sunset display and all the colours would spill through the soaring high-arched windows and bathe the ballroom in a tide of rose gold. Kerry and Zoe would dress at home and be flown to Castle Hill in the station helicopter an hour before the ceremony was to begin. Toni was picked up a little after one, allowing time for the bridesmaids to make themselves beautiful.

Cate, almost dancing in her joy and excitement, couldn't wait to show Toni the ballroom. "It looks absolutely beautiful," Toni exclaimed, her eyes moving around the huge paneled room. Its grandness had been softened by the extravagantly beautiful arrangements that illuminated every corner. The huge Chinese vases, part of an Oriental porcelain collection scattered all over the house, had been utilised to hold the white bridal flowers in tall stately arrangements. The twin fishbowls on carved stands that usually flanked the staircase defined the area where Bishop McGrath would stand, where masses and masses of white and pale green cymbidiums held up their magnificent spikes.

"It's a romantic fantasy." Toni sighed.

"And it took a lot of planning. Do you like the ribbons on the chairs?"

"Tied by an artist." Toni admired the large rosettes and flowing magnolia satin ribbons that graced the sides of the chairs on the aisle.

"Wait until you see the reception hall," Cate said in a happy, excited voice. "The whole venture has been an incredible success. Byrne's brain wave. I'll bet if we lived in the city we'd have a going concern with the complex. It's an ideal setting for a wedding, and it's so big it holds a huge crowd in comfort. You'll love what the decorators have done. They were worth every penny. When you get married, Toni, it would be wonderful if you could hold your wedding reception here. Your friends are our friends. Today we really become family." Spontaneously she gave Toni a hug, then saw Byrne entering the room, all lean, dark grace, with his beautiful smile, on this day of days, at the ready.

"Ah, there you are Cate," he said. "Hi, Toni, so you've arrived?"

"Safe and sound!" Everything about him made her giddy with pleasure. The sight, the sound, the way his silver eyes settled on her. And stayed.

"So I see." He transferred his attention to his sister. "Cate, Mamma wants you. Something about a flower girl's headdress."

"Oh, that would be Camille. I was just about to show Toni the hall. It's marvellous. Everyone has worked so hard."

"It's your big day, Cate." Byrne bent to kiss his sister's cheek.

"The whole idea of the old stables complex began with you. It's splendid, and I love and thank you for it. Show Toni over it, then she has to come upstairs to make herself beautiful."

"That shouldn't take long." Byrne's eyes were brilliantly, amusedly alive.

"If only Dad could be here," Cate said, dipping her dark gleaming head, already styled into a smooth classic look to suit her headpiece.

"He'll be here," Byrne assured her. "You'll feel him beside you even if I am giving you away."

Cate looked at him for a long moment. "You're the best brother in the world," she said gently, blinking to dispel one emotional tear.

"Thanks, Cate. It's just the sort of thing I want to hear." He smiled.

"I know, I know, it's cost a great deal of money."

He didn't consider that at all. "I want you to know making this day perfect for you is all that matters."

Soft and flushed with happiness, Cate turned to the door. "Well, I'd better go see to young Camille. She's as temperamental as a ballet dancer. Allow time for the hairdresser, Toni," she warned. "She's going to love fixing your hair."

"I hope she's not planning on doing too much," Byrne said when Cate had gone. His forehead creased with a touch of dismay. "I like it just the way it is. Long and thick and shining, radiating perfect health." Toni didn't need an elaborate hairdo to look stunning.

She smiled at his expression. "I expect she'll want to lift the front away from my face to complement the headdress, that's all. So stop looking like I'm going to finish with a lacquered beehive.''

"Tell her from me. I want you to look natural.''

"Okay, I promise.'' Toni moved into the centre of the room, half closing her eyes against the flood of light and the shimmering floral arrangements with their fresh, sweet perfume. ''This will be a glory when the afternoon sun pours through those high windows.''

He smiled as she moved into a beam of light. ''Which is just what Cate intended. I haven't had an opportunity to really speak to you since Zoe arrived home. She was absolutely charming the other night.''

"She said the same thing about you.''

"No one is disputing her good taste. It was an absolute coup, her coming up with your share of Nowra as a wedding present.'' His eyes were fixed on her with disconcerting steadiness. ''Of course, you didn't have anything to do with it?''

"Why should you say that?''

"Oh, I think I've got to know you pretty well. You have a healing touch, Antoinette. Kerry has been dogged by deep-seated...problems. Things from the past. It seemed to me they had eased. He looked very comfortable and caring with Zoe.''

Toni turned and walked to him, her manner showing her lightness of spirit. ''They've been getting on really well. Kerry had a confused idea Zoe didn't really love him. She does. But he has Cate now.''

"He's *always* had Cate.'' Byrne's eyes glinted with amusement.

"It's amazing, isn't it? For some people there is only that one special person.''

He took a while to answer. "Sometimes revelation comes right out of the blue."

"I know that too well."

He touched her cheek almost with reverence. "Toni, you haven't lived." She looked the very picture of innocence.

"I know all about heartbreak." She stared at him. "I know life is very short. I know love's a glory. I glory in you." She felt an odd sense of shock as the words spilled out.

"Toni, you don't." He drew her to him.

She leaned against him, turned her face into his shoulder. "I'm so sorry. That just popped out."

Why not? Hadn't he been guarding his tongue from her for some time? "In another year you might feel quite differently." He felt like an actor reciting some lines. What the hell was he trying to do? Drive her away?

"You make me weep, Byrne." She lifted her head, her beautiful violet eyes starry with unshed tears. "I'm the only one who can say who I'll love. If only it was like that with you."

Some part of him was exultant at her admission. "Antoinette, you're so *young*," he said with as much pain as principle. "*Too young* to make a forever commitment. That's the only kind of commitment I could ever accept."

"Which means you don't love me," she murmured sadly. "You want me now but you don't really see me in your life."

He winced. "You *are* in my life, Toni. Neither of us can change that." God forbid he should make her a prisoner. This creature of light. "What you're feeling is an adventure. I'm here to cut your teeth on. I'm Byrne

Beresford who has known you all your life. However much I want you, and I can't imagine you don't know it, I would always keep you safe. It's a heavy responsibility. There's a wedding going on. A heady time. Magic is abroad, like the mirage that turns a dry gully into an oasis.''

"You want me to go away?" Her eyes moved to his face.

"Toni, don't let me upset you. Not today. I care too much about you.''

"You're a strange man, Byrne Beresford,'' she said. "A woman could as soon tame you as an eagle.''

"You don't really want me tame, do you?''

His smile stopped her heart. She raised her head, all emotions and desires coming to the surface. "I want you to love me.'' She laughed, a brittle silvery sound. "Isn't that a joke?'' She jerked her slender body backward, coming up hard against his encircling arm, struggling a little, only he wasn't letting her go.

"Take that sad look off your face,'' he begged.

"I won't.'' Her eyes darkened to purple. "Why shouldn't I be sad? What's all this about, anyway?''

"Don't, Toni,'' he retorted too quietly. "You'd drive a man crazy.''

"That's funny, coming from you,'' she challenged. "Is that what I am for you, too? An adventure. A nice change from all the other women who come along. The women who worship you.''

"We don't need all this talk.'' His expression tautened.

"Then what do we need? Tell me.''

Passion was a high blue flame. It reached out for both of them and licked them. Not even Byrne could fight it.

This was life!

This was the stupendous feeling that made magic out of living. He held her fast, bending his head and taking her soft, furious mouth. She was excited, overwrought. He could feel the trembling right through her body. What did he want, anyway? He was mad with thinking about it. Nights of worrying and thinking about Antoinette Streeton. Nights of dreaming of having her in his bed. Her silvery blond hair splashed against his pillow. Her lovely spirited body his to love and know.

Did he want to marry her?

He *couldn't* marry her. She had to have a chance to choose properly. He knew he was controlling her. He knew he was hard and arrogant. This beautiful girl into woman. What would he do when she was gone?

He kissed her again and again until Toni went limp, nothing clear in her mind except she loved him with every atom of her being. He was cruel. He was exquisitely tender. Marvelously erotic.

"Aah." She sighed, her breath like a flowering. "How can I possibly forget you if you won't let me?"

A curious expression, half hard, half confounded, was written on his dark face. Forget him? He hated the sound of it. It made him feel cold, entirely alone in some strange, bleak landscape.

"You can't forget me," he said.

"I must." She was trying to pull away. "Why aren't you comfortable with the thought? You should be. Why do you let this go on?"

He looked nakedly into her violet eyes. "Because I can't stop it. That's the devil of it, Antoinette. I want you too much."

*   *   *

Everyone who attended the Streeton Beresford wedding would remember it as a most marvelous happy occasion, the wedding of the year. The bride, her bridesmaids and three little flower girls looked breathtaking as they started their stately glide down the long Persian carpet to where the groom and his attendants, resplendent in morning suits with black pleated trousers and dark gray striped silk cravats, were waiting. Bishop McGrath in his wedding vestments faced them, smiling, waiting to perform the ceremony that would unite two great pioneering families.

At four o'clock the wedding service began, and the murmurs became a swell as everyone turned to catch their first sight of the bride and her gorgeous entourage. Cate approached in her wonderful gown, a waist-length shimmering veil falling from her coronet of satin roses. Lustrous pearl drops, Kerry's gift, swung against her cheeks. Her blue eyes glowed in a face that was a little pale with emotion. Behind her were her bridesmaids, stunning each one, but none more dazzling than her chief bridesmaid in her blue-violet gown, her blond head crowned by a coronet of exquisite flowers that reflected the jewel colours of the bridesmaids' gowns. The enchanting flower girls seemed dazed by all the splendour, the decorated ballroom, the stately music, the sea of faces, the great chandeliers with their tiers of light and the candles on the long carved table that served as an altar. They looked adorable in their cream silk dresses with underskirts of tulle, pink roses catching the gathered skirt and the full puffed sleeves, posies in their hands and flowers and ribbons in their hair. They were cousins and best friends, mindful of this honour.

Toni felt her eyes fill with tears at her brother's smile

when he first caught sight of his bride. There was so much love in him. It shone from his soul.

May your love endure forever, Toni prayed silently as Bishop McGrath began the traditional Anglican service.

Before his final utterances and the pure notes of the boy soprano, who brought tears to many an eye, had faded away, sunset began to cascade through the soaring casements, flooding the assembly with magical light. There were smiles, nods, happy tears, soft spontaneous exclamations of delight. The bridegroom bent to kiss his bride, then the wedding march began with great aplomb, sweet, loud, full of the miracle of love. Kerry and Cate faced family and friends, their young faces transfigured by the overwhelming joy and significance of this, their wedding day.

Mr. and Mrs. Streeton.

Toni saw her mother touch a delicate lace-edged handkerchief to her eyes.

Only when the bridal couple had passed into the library did the homestead resound with exuberant cheers for the bride and groom.

"Such a happy day, darling," Zoe whispered to her daughter. Zoe was ravishing in an ice blue suit, sapphires and diamonds around her neck and at her ears, a chic little hat trimmed with a garland of flowers and a bewitching eye veil tipped forward on her forehead. "I just know in my heart you're going to be next."

The little flower girls, set free from the solemnity of the occasion, rushed about with glee, playing peekaboo behind the bridesmaids' billowing skirts and waving at the other beautifully dressed children. They all began to troop over to the reception with lots of exuberant hugs and shouted greetings along the way as old friends met up. Everyone professed amazement and delight at what had been achieved with the old stone stable. What a restoration!

A cousin turned to Byrne, half serious. "Can I book it now?"

The day was coming to a glorious end. The afternoon heat had completely lifted, and everyone, thanks to high emotion and delight in their surroundings, found themselves enormously hungry. Ready, in fact, for the great wedding feast that followed.

Byrne's speech, though short, filled them all with a pervading warmth. He spoke movingly of his sister and his family, then finished off with a funny little anecdote extolling Cate's very special virtues. They all laughed, and Sonia looked at her son, so splendid, so distinguished, his gray wool-mohair morning suit so beautifully cut, fitting his wide shoulders to perfection, the silver-gray silk of his striped cravat accentuating the luminous colour of his eyes. She was so proud of him. Sometimes she thought she couldn't stand it. This immense overflowing love.

By about eight o'clock the reception shifted into dance mode. The young people moved onto the polished floor, massing and swirling to the music of the excellent band. All the bridesmaids had removed their boleros to reveal their beautiful strapless gowns, and Joel, an expression of delight on his face, grabbed Toni, whirling her off into the midst of the extremely energetic dancers. Some, after one champagne too many, were openly smooching, others, so as not to be out of it, were dancing solo.

"It's all gone beautifully, hasn't it?" Joel said with great satisfaction. "I think I'm a little drunk. I suppose

I can be at my own sister's wedding. Doesn't she look marvellous? I've never seen her look anywhere near so good. It's true about brides." He looked toward the bridal couple, Cate's two arms locked around Kerry's neck. "You look gorgeous, too. Did I tell you?"

"About a dozen times." Toni smiled.

"Did you like Byrne's present to the attendants?"

"I don't think any of us expected such a gift," Toni answered simply. Byrne had presented them with beautiful jewelled broaches in the shape of a swan as a memento of this very special day. French perfume in lovely designer bottles from Cate. So much had been happening, Toni was certain no one had noticed that Andrea hadn't once directly addressed her. Oh, she was acting very friendly, very much into enjoying herself, but Toni knew Andrea was biding her time.

Nevertheless the suddenness of it took her by surprise. "I must speak to you," Andrea said, coming up behind Toni and laying a hand on her arm.

"Fine, go ahead." Toni turned, determined to be pleasant, meeting Andrea's green gaze steadily.

"Your mother is certainly beautiful," Andrea said, sounding surprised.

"Yes. Yes, she is." Toni had been keeping an eye on her mother. She was dancing with a tall, elegant grayhaired gentleman. Toni thought she knew him but couldn't place him.

"She's actually more stunning than I was led to believe."

"Paris," Toni responded in a light, dry voice. "It puts one on one's toes."

"It was good of her to come, but when is she going home?"

"When it suits her, Andrea."

There was silence as Andrea's emotions rose. "Well, Kerry will miss her. But I imagine you'll be returning to Paris together?"

"Certainly for a little while," Toni acknowledged. "We both have to put our affairs in order."

"You don't mean to say you're coming back?" Andrea showed her dismay.

"This is my home, isn't it?"

"You're not going to live with Kerry and Cate. That would be ludicrous."

Toni sought to put an end to the interrogation. "Andrea, I'm not yet sure of my plans. Why the interest?"

"You know darn well," Andrea said in a tight voice. "Byrne may be attracted to you now simply because you're beautiful, but he won't marry you."

"I don't think he's going to marry you, either, Andrea," Toni said, not unkindly.

"He hasn't married anyone else. Let's face it, he may see you as a passing fancy, but marriage, no. Surely you've seen the steel in him? He's not Joel, to be won over. He's an intensely serious man. He makes tough decisions all the time. He wouldn't risk a girl like you. But *our* relationship was working very well until you arrived."

Andrea walked away. Men often married women they didn't love, Toni thought, women who could play the necessary part. Byrne might well do the same.

She'd almost given up hope of dancing with him, perilous as that experience might be, but like the moth she was drawn to the flame. He was surrounded by people, men and women, all vying to capture his attention. Once he caught her eye and his handsome mouth compressed as if to say, *Well, I am stand-in father of the bride*. It must be tedious for him sometimes, being head of the clan, Toni thought. There was Joel, doing exactly what he pleased, his arm around Fern's shoulder while she looked at him with sweet intensity, an all-is-forgiven expression.

Toni was on the dance floor with Fern's attractive brother when Byrne cut in, wearing such a charm the birds-out-of-the-trees smile that James, who had waited patiently to claim a dance, relinquished Toni without a complaint.

"Only for you, Byrne," he murmured. "Toni, I'll claim you later, if I may?"

She forgot James entirely as Byrne gathered her close. As the evening progressed, the band's upbeat repertoire had given way to slow romantic tunes, the popular love songs of the day.

"You look wonderful. A vision of delight," he said after a few pulsing moments. His voice was low and, it seemed to her, faintly disturbed.

She wasn't sure. It was difficult to get *anything* into focus when he was holding her in his arms, pressing her against his lean body. Something Andrea had said to her stayed. The steel in him. The ability to take tough decisions.

She had to retain her poise. "Thank you, Byrne. Everything has gone marvellously well. You must be pleased."

"Mr. and Mrs. Streeton." He glanced in the bridal couple's direction. "Yes, I am pleased. Have you ever seen another couple so happy?"

"That's not our story," she said wryly. "Tomorrow

this sweet golden day will be over. I'll probably go back to Paris. You'll probably see a lot more of Andrea."

Deliberately he looked over the top of her ash-blond head with its lovely coronet of flowers. "I wish Andrea everything good in life, but it should be clear by now I have no romantic interest in her. Besides, I can't redirect my feelings so easily."

"Feelings pass. You told me yourself."

Stop it, Toni, she told herself sharply. She was provoking him, which could lead to danger. It was all the excitement, the champagne.

"You'd like me to give in to a grand passion?" he challenged.

"I'd like you to but I realise it would be too big a departure from yourself." What ambivalence was within her. Love and anger.

"But you wonder just the same?"

"Byrne, those kisses weren't fake," she said sadly. They had stolen her heart.

"You want the power to change my life."

Tension was a live wire. Touching him. Touching her. "You know what Tennyson said. "Tis better to have loved and lost than never to have loved at all.'"

He gave her a sharp smile. "We both know rapturous love affairs can end dreadfully. I would never wish a painful experience on you."

"A little bit late, isn't it?" She smiled over his shoulder at an old acquaintance.

"No way, Antoinette, I'd let *my* wife fly off."

A two-heartbeat pause. Heartbeats that hammered. "I don't doubt that for a moment." She had an acute sense of his iron resolve. "But why, if you love our world so much, do you see it as a prison?"

"It's a man's world, Toni. I don't have to caution you about that. The loneliness and isolation take their toll on women. Sooner or later many of them crack."

It was true. Marriages had suffered. Gone on the rocks. Her parents' among them. It wasn't enough to be in love. A station man spent a great deal of his time away from the homestead. The woman had to build a life for herself and her children. And when the children went away to boarding school? A woman's vulnerability was always exposed. The love bonds were everything. Nevertheless, there were those who managed splendidly. Wives, mothers, helpmates, community leaders.

She lifted her head. "You don't seem to have these worries about Cate."

"Cate has found her perfect connection," he said. "It has always been that way. In a sense Kerry needs Cate perhaps more than she needs him. Cate comes into the Earth Mother category."

"I agree. How do you see me?"

He looked at her in her exquisite finery. "You're closer to the stars than the earth. Hair like sunshine, eyes like the sky . The way you look today is an image I won't ever forget." It was said with such controlled passion, Toni felt the tears glitter in her eyes.

"Why do you say such sweet things to me?" she asked in a soft, perplexed voice. "Why do you look at me the way you do? Why do you hold me like this?"

"I told you. I haven't the strength not to."

"But tomorrow will put a stop to it?"

How could it? Every minute she was in his arms his desire for her was escalating. Soaring to an unbearable pitch. "Tomorrow might take us in different directions."

She gave a painful little intake of breath. "No, you'll

continue in the same old way. You're afraid of losing yourself.''

He didn't hesitate with his response. ''And you, Toni, are not afraid enough,'' he said harshly.

The revels went on into the early hours of the morning, long after the bridal couple had retired to the suite especially prepared for them. In the morning Byrne would fly them to a domestic terminal on the first leg of their honeymoon trip, which would take them first to the Great Barrier Reef to relax in the glorious sea and sun, then on to a whirlwind tour of southeast Asia with all its exotic delights, culminating in ten days on the island of Phuket. Three months in all. It was as long away from Nowra as Kerry felt comfortable with. During their absence the station foreman, Drew Hackett, a very capable man, would take over. Many of the guests were prepared to party until morning, when an early breakfast would be served for those who still had some room left for food.

Toni retired around two o'clock, after kissing Zoe good-night. Zoe was still firmly anchored to her new soul mate, the distinguished gray-haired gentleman who turned out to be Cornelius Grant, one of Beresford Enterprises' top executives. He had worked for the family for many years, which was why Toni had found his face familiar. Zoe seemed especially pleased to renew their acquaintance.

Will it ever end? Toni thought. At least Cornelius Grant was free, a widower for some years. Zoe wouldn't be outraging any wife.

In her bedroom she took off her wonderful gown and laid it over the daybed, adjusting the folds of the billow-

ing skirt. She didn't just feel tired. She felt exhausted.
Exhausted with emotion. How was she going to handle
the rest of her days? How was she going to handle tomorrow? A few of them were flying to the terminal to
see Cate and Kerry off.

In her nightdress and gown she wandered to the
French doors, then went onto the veranda to look toward
the stone complex, still brilliantly lit and still a hive of
activity. Outback people had enormous energies. And
how they loved big functions! It was perfectly understandable. They lived in such isolation, big gala occasions gave them an opportunity to let their hair down.
These occasions were to be enjoyed to the hilt. Normally
she would have been down there, too, but being so close
yet so far away from Byrne was a torment. Her pride
and her poise had been crumbling. She had been forced
to retreat.

The moon shone down on the station like a silver sun.
It was so radiant, it lit up the dark shadows. The music
poured from the hall, sweet soulful music that was part
of the night. Romantic music to serenade the young lovers. Sweet as it was, it put her nerves on edge. At that
moment she was *in pain,* her heart troubled. She had
returned home heart whole. Now she had lost it. In all
likelihood she would never get it back. She wasn't Zoe.
She was her father's daughter. Her feelings went very
deep.

Another thirty minutes passed. She couldn't sleep.
Mind and heart were in chaos. Hadn't he tried to warn
her? Hadn't he told her there was no sense in dreams?
She had made such a fool of herself. She had declared
her heart, and he had refused it. The humiliation seared.

She leaped up in the darkness and shouldered into the

jade silk robe Zoe had bought her. Maybe if she had the smallest nip of brandy it might help her sleep. Zoe often said a nip helped her. A few lights were left burning along the corridor to light the way for guests, but there was no one about. No sound within the great house. She would find what she was after in the library, a selection of spirits in crystal decanters. She was almost at the bottom of the staircase when her heart leaped into her throat like a fish from a stream.

"Oh, Byrne," she cried in excitement and anguish. "You startled me."

He looked at the young woman he held in his arms. "Ah, the sacrificial lamb," he said with mordant wit. He knew that she had fled him. Sought refuge in the house. It aroused punishing torments. Beneath the silk robe was a mere slip of a nightgown, luminous against the creamy skin of her body. He wanted so desperately to peel it away from her. His hand moved delicately, caressingly over her rose-peaked breast. For once he had drunk too much, using alcohol as a shield against the force of emotion. "Why wouldn't you stay at the reception?" he taunted her.

Hardly breathing, she leaned into his body, allowing his hand to continue the open exploration of her too lightly clad body. This was a seduction impossible to resist. The whole scene conspired against her, the night, the shadowy darkness, the sheer electric impact of contact with his body.

"Well?" He tongued the silky whorls of her ear.

"I was tired. It's very late." What were *words?*

"You had to escape me."

"I don't know that I have," she said shakily.

"I don't know that you could. Why are you wandering the house in little more than a silk veil?"

"I couldn't sleep, Byrne. That's the truth."

"So what were you after?" His mouth trailed her arched throat.

"Lord, I don't know." She swallowed hard against a wild surge of sensation, like surf in her ears. "A brandy, maybe."

"Brandy's not the answer," he said with deep certainty. "Take it from me."

He was, he knew, on the verge of giving way to his driving desires. At other times, all other times, he could have kept some control, but coming on her like this was too much. His senses were satiated with her. The sight and the scent. What was he supposed to be made of, granite? Years of self-discipline, striving to expand his self-reliance crumbled as a traitorous recklessness stole into his blood. The night was infinitely accommodating. The party would go on for all hours. He had excused himself by saying he was piloting Kerry and Cate in the morning. He had no plan to seek out Antoinette. He knew beyond doubt what that would mean, yet here she was in the most ravishing way imaginable. Waiting for him. Not consciously, maybe, but with the same wild longing fermenting in her blood. She wasn't even breathing on her own. She was breathing with him, staring at him through a shimmery sheen of tears.

It cut him to the heart, but it was too late. She wasn't going anywhere but to his bed. Nothing could protect her now. Certainly not him. It was the first real breakdown of his life.

He set her on his bed in the huge, moon-drenched room. It accepted her presence as totally as it accepted his. He seemed to be fighting for breath. He went to the heavy cedar door and turned the lock.

"You want me to make love to you, don't you?" His voice was so far from normal he scarcely recognised it. Gone was the hard control, the prized detachment. Yet if she sounded the least bit frightened or panicked, all the fire inside him would die.

Instead she lifted herself from the bed, wonderful shining hair spilling over her shoulders, arm outstretched. "You know I do," she said, unable, unwilling to suppress all the love that was in her.

A great weight lifted from him. In its place came exaltation. What life would be like married to this beautiful creature! To have that slender lovely body all the nights of his life. To give in to this wild craving.

"Byrne," she whispered when he lowered his lean, powerful body over hers. "Love me."

It was an appeal as old and poignant as time.

CHAPTER EIGHT

TONI had no clear recollection of seeing Cate and Kerry off. She was transfixed by the hours of ecstasy she had shared with Byrne. No experience of her life could ever surpass it, even then not fully realising Byrne's indomitable passion for her. He had taken her, body and soul, searing into her the print of his flesh. It was rapture that left her consumed, dissolved in tears he had kissed away.

"Hush, my little love," he had whispered, "steady," while her body, made perfect by his passion, trembled violently in the exquisite aftermath.

She awoke cradled in his arms and he took her again, breaking her heart. This was love. She didn't need to speak it, though he had crooned to her, murmured to her, cuddled her close to him for a long, long time. He had taken her to her room, knowing she was still lost in the dream they had shared.

They saw no one. Breakfast was already being served to the revellers who had partied the night through. In another hour the sun would climb right up into the sky. Another day would begin. *Another day.* When she felt herself changed forever.

Zoe, who had behaved marvellously well, sweet and gracious to everyone present, mercifully withholding her great talent for flirtation, decided almost immediately she wanted to return to Paris.

"You promised me you'd come back with me, darling." Zoe looked at her daughter uncertainly. "What's the matter with you, anyway? You seem in a daze. That's not like you at all.''

Toni felt the traitorous blood rush to her face.

"Oh, Lord!" Zoe stopped her packing and sank onto the bed. "It's Byrne, isn't it? You slept with him.''

"That's my business, Mamma.''

"Don't be too sure. You chase enough of my admirers off." Zoe leaned over and took her daughter's hand. "How was it?''

"Mamma." Toni started to protest again.

"All right, I know." Zoe laughed. "It's written all over you. Sensational. So what happens now?''

"I have absolutely no idea. He hasn't offered to marry me, if that's what you're expecting.''

Zoe went back to her folding. "Then what exactly does he think he's doing, trying to break my little girl's heart?''

Toni pressed into the cushioned armchair. "It was perfect, Mamma. He's perfect," she said softly.

Zoe smiled a little sadly. "I could have guessed that. You'd better come to Paris with me. We'll settle our affairs. It will give you both a breathing space. Byrne plays his hand pretty close to his chest, but even he can't hide the fact he's fallen head over heels in love with you. I'd say you're the best thing that has ever happened to him. He needs your special sweetness in his life. Your kind of loving.''

"Tell him, Mamma." Toni had to laugh.

"No, darling, it's true. You've sustained me through thick and thin. You worked so hard to look after me and my interests. No one, not even your father, showed such concern. It's been wonderful, my reconciliation with Kerry. He and Cate went off so happy. I love him dearly, but I can't pretend you're not my favourite child. You accept me completely whatever I am.''

Some note in her mother's voice, some bleak recognition of failure, got Toni to her feet. She disengaged herself from the pile of cushions, went over to Zoe and kissed her. "You're my *mother*. One word, but it describes all the love in the world.''

A day later, when Byrne flew the helicopter to Nowra, Zoe gave them privacy, explaining she had packing. "I'll be back in half an hour or so.'' She smiled at Byrne charmingly. "We'll have coffee.'' They were alone, but Toni found it difficult to speak. She could not dismiss the memory of those hours together. It seemed to hold her and her tongue captive.

"So what have you decided to do?'' Byrne asked finally, his eyes on her dreamy flushed face. She wore her beauty so carelessly because it was all so natural. No makeup on her flawless skin. A light gloss of lipstick, her beautiful hair pulled into a tight ballerina-like topknot. A blue tank top like a second skin, white linen shorts that showcased her long, golden legs. He almost contemplated picking her up, bundling her into the helicopter and flying away. Somewhere with a white beach, turquoise surf, swaying palms. Somewhere no one could hunt him down. Where he didn't have to make decisions at every turn. Where he could close a door. Concentrate on Antoinette. Make passionate love to her.

"Zoe wants me to go to Paris with her. Finalise our affairs,'' Toni said, watching a flight of white corellas settle in the trees.

"She intends to return then?''

"She's ready to leave Europe,'' Toni said, happy

about the decision. "She thinks she might buy a smart harbourside apartment in Sydney."

"She'll be paying a fortune." Byrne's tone was dry.

"Claude was very good to her."

"In turn, she's been good to you and Kerry." He nodded.

"Everything has worked out well," Toni said with satisfaction.

"And you had nothing to do with it?"

"I suggested solutions." She looked at his beloved face, looked away.

"How?"

Tears sprang into her eyes. "Tell me you love me."

He reached for her hand, lifted it, kissed. "Don't look like that, Toni."

"Is it better if I smile?"

"Your tears bring me undone," he responded almost crisply. "We're not on our own, though Zoe has been very diplomatic leaving us alone."

"I can't forget the other night." Her face took on a look of soft wonder.

"Tell me you'll never regret it."

"Regret it," she repeated incredulously. She shook her head as though the remembrance was too great. "I *do* love you, Byrne."

"And you'll never love anyone else?" he asked, voice light, eyes intense.

"What do you want me to say?"

"Never?" he persisted. "Because I'd never let *you* go. You with the huge violet eyes looking at me so desperately. Don't you know it was the same for me?"

She looked away, remembering the things he had said to her. "Yes," she whispered.

They were silent for a while, emotion a deep under-current.

"It might seem very hard, but I'd like you to go with Zoe. Do what you have to do. Get your bearings. When you're ready, come home," Byrne said finally, as though making up his mind.

It was shocking. Nothing like she had been expecting. "Then you're letting me go."

"Giving you a free rein is central to everything."

It was astounding, the ease with which passion could turn to anger. "Obviously it's better for you if I go away?" She didn't know how to channel all the tumultuous emotion their coming together had undammed.

"No, I don't like it at all," he replied bluntly, "but you'll think better."

"What about?" She shivered at the dazzling sparkle in his eyes. "I need no time to think."

He studied her highly expressive young face. "You do. Just for a little while. There's been an excess of emotion all these weeks. The wedding has been a tremendous stimulant. We both know that. I want you to come down to earth for a little while."

"You don't trust my love for you? Is that it? You don't trust anyone, Byrne."

"You're not fully understanding my line of reasoning. You know so much, but you've got much to learn. Don't make it hard for us both. This is a short separation so you can get a true understanding of your feelings."

"You mean a perspective of love?" She gave a brittle laugh.

"Look at you," he said gently. "You know you're emotional."

"Why wouldn't I be, after what happened?" Her anger abated as quickly as it had begun. She clasped her hands, folded them neatly in her lap. "Shall we have coffee?" she suggested, too brightly. "I've even made a chocolate cake."

"Then I *must* have it."

Toni sprang gracefully to her feet. "It's so pleasant when people drop in."

Even love has its sharp edges.

Byrne never did call from Australia. He wrote. Long, newsy letters growing in size. She couldn't pretend they were love letters, yet they had such a sense of immediacy she felt he was in the room with her. As well as keeping her up to date on what was happening at home, he gave her plenty of advice. All excellent big-brother stuff. In fact, the sort of thing she had once longed for from Kerry but never got. If she didn't know better she would have thought that unforgettable night they shared was pure fantasy. Fantasy bred of playing with fire. Sometimes at night slow tears of frustration rolled down her cheeks. Missing Byrne was an agony.

It took Zoe a lot longer than expected to say goodbye to her friends, sell the apartment and finalize her affairs. When they were deciding on dates to return to Australia Claude suffered a mild heart attack. Since the breaking up of their marriage Claude had returned to his wonderful sixteenth-century manor house in the Loire Valley, but he and Zoe were constantly in touch. Now that they had gone their separate ways they were friendlier than ever. Claude, twenty years Zoe's senior, was genuinely fond of her, but he hadn't been able to keep pace with her abundant energy and sexual demands. Now that he didn't have to, all the tensions had eased. At the news

Zoe immediately packed a bag to go to him. "Are you sure you won't come with me, darling?" she implored. "Claude is so fond of you. I'm sure he's going to leave you something in his will."

"I don't want anything from his will, Mamma," Toni said faintly. "Give him my love and tell him I wish him a speedy recovery."

Would she ever understand her mother? Now that they had broken up, Zoe and Claude were practically inseparable. The big thing with Zoe was to make her laugh, and Claude could tell wonderful stories in four different languages.

By Saturday, Zoe hadn't returned from the shelter of the manor's ancient walls but she had rung each day with a report on Claude's progress. Mercifully, Claude was in no danger. "A little warning to be heeded," Zoe said. He didn't want Zoe to return to Australia, but she promised him she would spend time with him each year. Claude really knew how to live, Zoe said. Good food, marvelous wine, the cigars he couldn't give up, which had brought on his heart attack, of course, Toni thought.

Left alone, she decided to accept an invitation to have dinner with a party of young friends, but at the last minute declined to go on to a nightclub. That's what Byrne had done to her. She couldn't think of anything or anyone else. Terrible pining kept gnawing away at her. If she was absolutely honest she would have to admit she wasn't enjoying anything very much. She could go home without Zoe, of course. Living in the wonderful romantic city of Paris, one of the great experiences of her life, she was lonely and bored. Every little fiber of her longed for a man with silver-gray eyes and black hair, a man who made the very air shiver with his vivid presence.

Her friends, still trying to change her mind, dropped her off outside her apartment building. She wasn't inside more than ten minutes when the doorbell rang, startling her. It had to be Zoe. No one else could get in. Security in the building was tight. Trust Zoe not to let her know she was coming.

When she opened the door, the shock stopped her breath.

Byrne stood on the threshold, a smile on his stunning face, at least two dozen red roses in the crook of his arm.

"Well, aren't you going to ask me in?" he asked as casually as if they had never been apart. "Or are you suffering from violent shock?"

She tried to laugh, did not succeed. "Byrne, it *is* you?"

"As I live and breathe." He moved closer, bent his dark head, put his mouth very briefly over hers.

She rested against the door for a moment, taking a deep breath. "Please come in. I'm just so surprised." In fact she felt hot and light, as though she could float.

"This is a very beautiful apartment, Antoinette," he said, glancing around.

"Claude gave it to Zoe when they were first married." She spoke rapidly. "She's sold it but settlement will take another few weeks. She's with Claude at the moment. He suffered a minor heart attack but he's on the mend."

"That's good," Byrne responded automatically, turning to her and holding out the roses. He was wearing a beautifully cut gray suit, an elegant red silk tie and a pale blue shirt. He looked stunning. "Toni?" he prompted gently.

"I'm sorry." She moved forward immediately.

"You've taken me so much by surprise. I'm not sure I'm not hallucinating." Excitement was overloading her nerve centres. She took the roses, went to find vases, distributed them between two big crystal bowls.

"Here, let me help you." Byrne took one vase from her while she went to fetch the other.

"They're so beautiful," she said. "Thank you." For a moment she buried her face in the fragrant crimson petals. "Tell me, how did you get in? Georges is very strict about security."

"I told him I was your friend from Australia," he explained. "The roses clinched it. I've been ringing most of the evening."

"I was out with friends." She spoke nervously, still battling the overload of excitement.

"You look gorgeous." Under his smooth banter was a powerful pounding. "But surely you've lost weight?"

"I'm into a rigorous exercise program," she joked.

"You'd better cancel it. You're bordering on fragile." He allowed his eyes to move over her. She was wearing a short, very sexy evening dress in a dull gold with some sort of a low draped bodice and a wide lace hem that revealed her lovely legs. She had certainly acquired Parisian panache.

"Please, Byrne, sit down. Could I get you anything?"

"Sure could," he said.

She couldn't look away. "What?"

"Tell me why you're so damned nervous?" He lowered his tall frame onto one of the sofas upholstered in Louis blue brocade.

"You make me feel like this all the time."

"Miss me?" There was a sparkle of devilment in his light eyes.

"Would I offend you if I said I've been very busy?"

"That's okay. I've been busy, too. Tell the truth."

"I've missed you terribly," she said in a rush. "But thank you so much for your letters. They told me everything—except whether you missed me."

"Why else would I be here, Antoinette?" He stood, scattering a charge of electricity over the beautiful, traditional room. "If the mountain won't come to Mohammed..."

"You're so cruel," she said before he caught her to him, kissing her mouth, reveling in its seductive shape.

"Did you dream about me?" He carried her to the sofa, cradled her across his knees.

A trace of tears glinted in her violet eyes, though she was smiling. "When I finally gave in to sleep, yes. Oh, Byrne, I'm just so overjoyed to see you."

"Then do you think you might show me?"

She lifted her slender arms, locked them around his neck, saw the faint lines of tension on his handsome dark face. "Not until you tell me you've punished me enough."

"Punish?" He groaned. "God, you were with me wherever I went. My first thought, my last thought and most in between. Nothing means a damned thing without you. You've moved right up under my heart."

She started to grit her small white teeth in an effort not to lose control, but the tears started to fall.

"Darling, you don't have to cry about it." He hugged her to him.

"You always manage to bring tears to my eyes. I love you so much."

"Then you'd better marry me," he suggested with extraordinary tenderness.

Her whole body turned incandescent. "You *mean* it?"

His love for her leaped like a flame. "I've come half-way across the world."

"And I was coming home to you. Without Zoe, if I had to. I can't be anywhere you're not."

"So I take it that's a yes?" he asked.

It was a wonderful moment, a moment she would never forget. "Yes," she whispered.

"'Let's seal it with a kiss. A life of joy in one another, Antoinette."

"Amen."

It was a long time before they spoke again.

Byrne twisted his lithe body, withdrew a small box from the pocket of his jacket, which he had draped over a chair. "The most time-honoured gesture of a man to his fiancée." He lifted her left hand and kissed it.

In the navy velvet box was a glorious ring. A large, square-cut sapphire of beautiful clarity and colour surrounded by a wreath of diamonds.

"What else but a sapphire for a woman with such eyes," Byrne said.

EPILOGUE

IT WAS the year of Beresford marriages, the gossip columns wrote, four in all, but none more newsworthy than the wedding of Byrne Beresford, chairman of Beresford Enterprises, cattle baron from legendary Castle Hill Station and arguably the country's most eligible bachelor, to Miss Antoinette Streeton, only daughter of the beautiful and popular society figure Zoe LeClair and the late Eric Streeton of Nowra Station.

The columns went on to say the bride was already halfway family, as her brother, Kerry, had married the bridegroom's sister earlier in the year. Unlike that splendid and lavish occasion, Mr. Beresford and Miss Streeton had chosen a quieter ceremony. The family fairly dripped money, so the low-key occasion came as a surprise to many, but it was clearly what the couple, said to be deliriously happy, wanted. Miss Streeton was to have three attendants—her sister-in-law, Catherine, matron of honour, a lifelong friend, Miss Fiona Crawford, and a Mademoiselle Dominique Dupré, who was flying in from Paris, where the bride had spent several years. Every society journalist in the country was desperate to get an invitation, but only one was sent, to the doyenne Fleur Colwyn of "Fleur's Diary."

"Low-key or not, it's bound to be gorgeous!" Fleur gushed to her editor, which, as a prediction, proved marvellously correct.

* * *

It had been a blazing hot day but the night was wondrously cool, the velvet dome of the sky a sweeping, star-studded glory. There were one hundred guests waiting for her outside, family, friends, people who were close to her. Ever since she could remember, Toni had dreamed of a wedding under the Southern Cross. She knew that was what she would have. When she had told Byrne of her special wish, to her joy he had found the idea delightful, so a starlight pageant it had become. Beautiful, memorable, imaginative.

After several pleasurable discussions, an amphitheatre had been decided on. Erected in Castle Hill's home gardens, it transformed the great glade of lawn—dominated by magnificent old gums and dense plantings, at the far end a lake filled with water lilies, irises, the huge gunneras and a flotilla of black swans—into an open-air temple. Hundreds of star lanterns were hung in the great trees, the fluted white columns were wreathed in exquisite white flowers, and ivy leaves trailed from top to bottom. An altar table of pristine marble stood on the wide dais flanked by two sandstone pedestals supporting large garden urns filled with masses and masses of luminous fragrant flowers. The raised floor of the amphitheatre was covered in a carpet especially woven for the wedding. It featured a large central star motif.

Toni's wedding dress was something out of a midsummer night's dream, a slender flute of white chiffon over silk, the low round neck and the long sheer sleeves embroidered with silver crystals with a river of glittering silver, ice blue and gold stars swirling diagonally across the ankle-length skirt. Around her neck she wore Byrne's exquisite gift to her, a necklace of two interlocking silver chains so arranged that the large and smaller diamonds strung along them formed an outline of the Southern Cross. A high rounded headband studded with diamanté secured her froth of a short veil with scatter sequins, diamond stud earrings at her ears. She was carrying a bridal posy of massed pink, cream and white roses interspersed with orchids and sprigs of fernery. On her feet she wore custom-made evening sandals, with three diamanté straps.

"You look too beautiful to be true. Like a young goddess," Zoe said tremulously, a vision in a couture outfit of aqua and apple green patterned silk, complemented by a stunning little veiled hat.

"I feel every inch a woman, Mamma." Toni's smile was radiant. A woman eager to go to her beloved, to be joined in holy matrimony before God and man.

For years after, people spoke about the Beresford wedding. The slender tapers the guests held that lighted the bride's procession. The beauty and radiance of the bride, the irresistible appeal of her star dress, the fiery pride of her groom, resplendent in a silver gray brocade Nehru jacket and gray trousers, his soft white shirt highlighted by a burgundy silk cravat. Could anything have been more magical, more summery than the open-air temple, a billion stars blossoming over them, the air so fresh, faces gilded in the flickering tapers, the shining teardrops, the sighs of absolute delight as the bride came into sight, followed by her attendants in lovely slim gowns of celeste blue, sugar pink and lime green silk, the bodices that winked in the candlelight encrusted with crystals and seed pearls? The music was perfect, too, Handel, Bach, Beethoven's "Ode to Joy," Elgar, carrying far and wide across the boronia-scented bushland to the silent, mysterious desert with its towering sand pyramids. And afterward, to cap the stylish reception, the most wonderful display of fireworks for the whole station to enjoy.

At the altar before Bishop McGrath, Byrne turned his blazing eyes to his bride, consumed by her beauty and his ever-burgeoning love for her. She was enchanting inside and out. Her lovely face, turned to him, rivalled the radiance of the stars. He knew he would remember her at this moment for the rest of his life. With a great sense of happiness and security in the woman he loved, Byrne turned as Bishop McGrath began the service that would make him and his beautiful Antoinette husband and wife.

Sometimes, if one was lucky, happiness was right on the doorstep....

**Head Down Under for twelve tales of heated
romance in beautiful and untamed Australia!**

**Here's a sneak preview of the first novel in
THE AUSTRALIANS**

Outback Heat by Emma Darcy
available July 1998

'HAVE I DONE something wrong?' Angie persisted, wishing Taylor would emit a sense of camaraderie instead of holding an impenetrable reserve.

'Not at all,' he assured her. 'I would say a lot of things right. You seem to be fitting into our little Outback community very well. I've heard only good things about you.'

'They're nice people,' she said sincerely. Only the Maguire family kept her shut out of their hearts.

'Yes,' he agreed. 'Though I appreciate it's taken considerable effort from you. It is a world away from what you're used to.'

The control Angie had been exerting over her feelings snapped. He wasn't as blatant as his aunt in his prejudice against her but she'd felt it coming through every word he'd spoken and she didn't deserve any of it.

'Don't judge me by your wife!'

His jaw jerked. A flicker of some dark emotion destroyed the steady power of his probing gaze.

'No two people are the same. If you don't know that, you're a man of very limited vision. So I come from the city as your wife did! That doesn't stop me from being an individual in my own right.'

She straightened up, proudly defiant, furiously angry with the situation. 'I'm *me*. Angie Cordell. And it's time you took the blinkers off your eyes, Taylor Maguire.'

Then she whirled away from him, too agitated by the explosive expulsion of her emotion to keep facing him.

The storm outside hadn't yet eased. There was nowhere to go. She stopped at the window, staring blindly at the torrential rain. The thundering on the roof was almost deafening but it wasn't as loud as the silence behind her.

'You want me to go, don't you? You've given me a month's respite and now you want me to leave and channel my energies somewhere else.'

'I didn't say that, Angie.'

'You were working your way around it.' Bitterness at his tactics spewed the suspicion. 'Do you have your first choice of governess waiting in the wings?'

'No. I said I'd give you a chance.'

'Have you?' She swung around to face him. 'Have you really, Taylor?'

He hadn't moved. He didn't move now except to make a gesture of appeasement. 'Angie, I was merely trying to ascertain how you felt.'

'Then let me tell you your cynicism was shining through every word.'

He frowned, shook his head. 'I didn't mean to hurt you.' The blue eyes fastened on hers with devastating sincerity. 'I truly did not come in here to take you down or suggest you leave.'

Her heart jiggled painfully. He might be speaking the truth but the judgements were still there, the judgements that ruled his attitude towards her, that kept her shut out of his life, denied any real sharing with him, denied his confidence and trust. She didn't know why it meant so much to her but it did. It did. And the need to fight for justice from him was as much a raging torrent inside her as the rain outside.

Harlequin Romance®

Everyone has special occasions in their life.
Maybe an engagement, a wedding, an anniversary, the
birth of a baby. Or even a personal milestone—a
thirtieth or fortieth birthday!

**These are times of celebration and excitement,
and we're delighted to bring you
a special new series called...**

The BIG Event

**One special
occasion—
that changes
your life
forever!**

We'll be featuring one terrific book each month,
starting in May 1998...

May 1998—BABY IN A MILLION
by Rebecca Winters (#3503)
June 1998—BERESFORD'S BRIDE
by Margaret Way (#3507)
July 1998—BIRTHDAY BRIDE
by Jessica Hart (#3511)
August 1998—THE DIAMOND DAD
by Lucy Gordon (#3515)

Look in the back pages of any *Big Event* book to find
out how to receive a set of sparkling wineglasses.

Available wherever Harlequin books are sold.

From the high seas to the
Scottish Highlands,
when a man of action
meets a woman of spirit
a battle of wills—
and love—ensues!

Ransomed Brides

This June, bestselling authors Patricia Potter and
Ruth Langan will captivate your imagination with this
swashbuckling collection. Find out how two men of action
are ultimately tamed by two feisty women who prove
to be *more* than their match in love and war!

SAMARA by Patricia Potter

HIGHLAND BARBARIAN
by Ruth Langan

Available wherever Harlequin and Silhouette
books are sold.

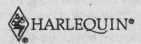

HARLEQUIN®   Silhouette®

Catch more great

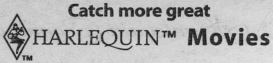

HARLEQUIN™ Movies

featured on the movie channel tmc

Premiering June 13th
Diamond Girl

based on the novel by bestselling
author Diana Palmer

Don't miss next month's movie!
Premiering July 11th
Another Woman
starring Justine Bateman and
Peter Outerbridge
based on the novel by Margot Dalton

If you are not currently a subscriber to
The Movie Channel, simply call your
local cable or satellite provider for more
details. Call today, and don't miss out
on the romance!

the movie channel tmc   ◆ **HARLEQUIN®**
Makes any time special ™

100% pure movies.
100% pure fun.

PHMBPA698

ℋarlequin ℛomance®

Coming Next Month

#3511 BIRTHDAY BRIDE Jessica Hart

Sexy, glamorous... Claudia tried to think of three good things about turning thirty. Having to pretend to be David Stirling's bride wasn't one of them. But for the next few weeks she was stuck with him and the pretense. And perhaps, at her age, sexy, glamorous and *wed* was an improvement?

We're delighted to bring you a special new series in Harlequin Romance and Presents all about...

The Big Event! *One special occasion—that changes your life forever.*

#3512 A KISS FOR JULIE Betty Neels

Julie enjoyed her work as a medical secretary, so it was a nasty surprise when her elderly boss announced he was retiring. She was partly reassured when told that Professor Simon van der Driesma was willing to keep her on—but Simon turned out to be a very different proposition....

#3513 THE BACHELOR AND THE BABIES Heather MacAllister

When Harrison Rothwell is left holding his brother's baby—well, two babies to be exact—he decides to demonstrate that his rules of business management can be applied to any situation. Trouble is, his tiny nephews won't take orders from any boss! Which is where Carrie Brent comes in. She may be totally disorganized but when it comes to rug rats—she's a natural! Can she convince Harrison that rules are made to be broken?

Get ready to meet the world's most eligible bachelors: they're sexy, successful and, best of all, they're all yours!

Bachelor Territory: *There are two sides to every story...and now it's his turn!*

#3514 LAST CHANCE MARRIAGE Rosemary Gibson

After one disastrous marriage, Clemency Adams had vowed to give up men and concentrate on her career. Her next-door neighbor, Joshua Harrington, was equally determined not to marry again. Unfortunately, these new neighbors were finding it difficult to fight their growing attraction for one another....